More Confessions
OF A
HOLLYWOOD
STARLET

Also by Lola Douglas

True Confessions of a Hollywood Starlet

More Confessions
OF A
HOLLYWOOD
STARLET

A NOVEL BY

LOLA DOUGLAS

razor
bill

More Confessions of a Hollywood Starlet

RAZORBILL

Published by the Penguin Group
Penguin Young Readers Group
345 Hudson Street, New York, New York 10014, U.S.A.
Penguin Group (USA) Inc., 375 Hudson Street, New York, New York 10014, U.S.A.
Penguin Group (Canada), 90 Eglinton Avenue, Suite 700, Toronto, Ontario, Canada M4P 2Y3 (a division of Pearson Penguin Canada Inc.)
Penguin Books Ltd, 80 Strand, London WC2R 0RL, England
Penguin Ireland, 25 St Stephen's Green, Dublin 2, Ireland
(a division of Penguin Books Ltd)
Penguin Group (Australia), 250 Camberwell Road, Camberwell, Victoria 3124, Australia (a division of Pearson Australia Group Pty Ltd)
Penguin Books India Pvt Ltd, 11 Community Centre, Panchsheel Park, New Delhi – 110 017, India
Penguin Group (NZ), 67 Apollo Drive, Rosedale, North Shore 0632, New Zealand (a division of Pearson New Zealand Ltd.)
Penguin Books (South Africa) (Pty) Ltd, 24 Sturdee Avenue, Rosebank, Johannesburg 2196, South Africa

Penguin Books Ltd, Registered Offices: 80 Strand, London WC2R 0RL, England

10 9 8 7 6 5 4 3 2 1

Interior design by Christopher Grassi

LIBRARY OF CONGRESS HAS CATALOGED THE HARDCOVER EDITION AS FOLLOWS:

Douglas, Lola.
  More true confessions of a Hollywood starlet / by Lola Douglas.
    p. cm.
  Summary: When her true identity as a Hollywood starlet is revealed, seventeen-year-old Morgan Carter, a recovering alcoholic and drug addict, must choose whether to return to her glamorous movie star existence or stick with the wholesome life, and the new love, she has found in the Midwest. Told in the form of diary entries.
  ISBN 1-59514-051-4
  [1. Actors and actresses—Fiction. 2. Celebrities—Fiction. 3. Drug abuse—Fiction. 4. Alcoholism—Fiction. 5. Diaries—Fiction.] I. Title.

  PZ7.D74737Mo 2006
  [Fic]—dc22

                                                                    2006019049

Razorbill paperback ISBN: 978-1-59514-129-3

Printed in the United States of America

I believe that everything happens for a reason, but I think it's important to seek out that reason—that's how we learn.
—Drew Barrymore

Week
THIRTEEN

11/9

Just got back from Chicago, a two-day quickie trip to make my first TV appearance since I was "outed" exactly one month ago today. Sam is still tweaked that I insisted on *Oprah* even after *60 Minutes* begged for an exclusive, but there's something about that Katie Couric that totally freaks me out. I mean, she *seems* nice enough, but her eternal perkiness is more cloying than Mama Bianca's $250 bottle of Shalimar perfume.

Frankly, if anyone should be tweaked, it's *me*. Sam failed to warn me that Bianca would be at the taping. And yes, I understand that he's Bianca's husband now, but he's still my manager, and after all these years, you'd think he'd show at least a *little* loyalty to his favorite client–turned-stepdaughter.

But that's another entry entirely.

Can I tell you how much I love Oprah? Not only did she leave this gorgeous, buttery, red leather journal and an assortment of her favorite Philosophy bath and beauty products in my dressing room, she also made sure to come down pre-taping to say hello. That, and to tell me that she appreciates me sharing my story with her audience. "Truly inspiring," quoth O.—and she wasn't all fake about it either, like a certain large-chinned late-night talk show host I can't stand who's *still* cracking farm girl jokes at my expense. No, she actually *meant* what she said.

Oh, but the best part? Oprah surprised me during the interview with all these lovely videotaped messages of encouragement from people like Drew Barrymore, Corey Feldman, and this old-school actress Tatum O'Neal—fellow former child stars who, like me, triumphed over their drug and alcohol addictions. It was almost as nice as the thousands of cards, letters, and care packages I received when news broke that I'd been hiding out at Fort Wayne, Indiana's, own Snider High.

I have to admit, though, that I hope my eventual comeback is more like Drew's than Corey's. I mean, hello! *Duplex* wasn't great art, but it's a hell of a lot better than becoming a cast member on *The Surreal Life*.

Speaking of, that dude who co-created *The Real World* left like a dozen messages on the machine while we were away. Apparently, Mr. Jonathan Murray has this idea that I could be the next big reality TV star. "Just like Paris and Nicole!" he kept saying, as if that was some sort of incentive. He's not the only one who's come sniffing around either. But hi—doesn't *anyone* get it? These days I'm trying to get *away* from the spotlight, not run farther into it.

Back to *Oprah*: Trudy came to Chicago with me as my chaperone, and everyone kept mistaking her for my mother. It made us giggle and Mama Bianca frown, but what does she expect? Trudy's been more of a mom to me these past several months than Bianca has been these past several *years*. Although I have to give Mama B. credit for trying: she's still begging me to meet her and Sam at some tropical location for Christmas. I told her I'd think about it if she and Sam would come to Indiana for Thanksgiving. Her perfectly collagen-plumped lips frowned; I knew she was counting on doing Turkey Day California style (read: nab invite to cushy catered dinner at celebrity couple's mansion *or* throw similar cushy catered dinner at one's own abode).

We'll just see about that, won't we?

I'd wanted to bring the twins to Chi-town for my *Oprah* appearance, too. After all, they were the best friends I'd made since I moved to the Fort. And they'd been awesome to me even when they didn't know I was really Morgan Carter. But Emily has some big project going at church, and there's no way Mrs. Whitmarsh was going to let Eli come with me without his sister's protection. She's been rather wary of me as of late, especially when it comes to her son. I guess I can't blame her entirely; after all, she *did* catch me sleeping in Eli's bed the morning after the news about my true identity broke.

It didn't quite matter that Eli had been a total gentleman and slept on the floor. I think it was the shock of finding *any* girl in her little boy's bed, especially since Eli was still using these ghastly kiddie sheets from one of the newer Star Wars movies.

Actually, if Mrs. Whitmarsh stopped to think about it, she would realize those sheets were, like, an anti-aphrodisiac. I mean, who wants to hook up on top of a cartoonified version of Natalie Portman's pseudo-geisha face?

Anyway, where was I? Oh, right—*Oprah*.

Except I just looked at the clock and realized that I'd better power down for the night. Oprah or no Oprah, if I don't show up for first-period geometry tomorrow, Mrs. Chappelle's going to kick my hypotenuse but good.

Can't sleep. Too wired from *Oprah*, or maybe it's that grande Sumatra that I picked up at O'Hare while Tru and I were waiting for our flight to board. According to *Teen Vogue*, caffeine addiction is the new high school epidemic.

I'm sorry, but after kicking booze, pills, pot, and all manner of snortable substances, a coffee jones is the *least* of my worries.

These past few weeks have been such a blur. At first it was fun, you know, getting to ditch Claudia's chunky glasses, sensible shoes, and lackluster style—not to mention her blander-than-bland brown hair. (Bianca insisted I color it immediately, and for once, I was in total agreement.) The deep red I now sport is a far cry from my former trademark blond, but even Mama B. admits that it suits the new me. It says serious. It says *survivor*.

Too bad she's keeping the bulk of my California wardrobe hostage—"It makes for better press if you keep wearing Old Navy," she explained, "like you really *are* just an average teenager"—as I have several Anna Sui pieces in varying shades of blue that would look smashing against my crushed-cherry-colored waves. Oh, well.

The truth is, I'm almost nostalgic for the days of attending Snider as Claudia Miller, average American high school student. "Claudia" could roll out of bed fifteen minutes before first bell and not worry about sleep hair or a lack of makeup. *She* could float from class to class in a fairly anonymous fashion. *She* had the luxury of privacy, something I'd otherwise never known.

And honestly? I wish I'd been more prepared to be Morgan Carter again. I mean, I'd spent six full paparazzi-free months in rehab at Crapplewood before being whisked into Indiana obscurity.

After the outing . . . well, let's just say it's been tanta-mount to a night of clubbing in Hollywood with Lindsay Lohan *and* Nicole Richie. I'm out of practice—you know, in terms of evading the stalkerazzi—and I've seen so many flashbulbs in the past thirty days that I'm surprised I haven't gone permanently blind.

I'd hoped that school might become a haven of sorts since Principal Barke was so adamant that no hacks be allowed on campus. But my classmates have been even *worse*.

At first, most of them gawked at me like I was a rare albino liger on exhibit at the Fort Wayne Children's Zoo. Then came the questions: did I know Brad Pitt/Ashton Kutcher/Ben Affleck/insert name of male hottie here? Was it true that I'd had a lesbian fling with my best friend (and current "it girl"), Marissa Dahl? When I OD'd outside the Viper Room, did the ghost of River Phoenix appear to me, telling me to run into the light?

Then there were those intrepid souls who snapped surrep-titious shots of me with their camera phones and e-mailed the images to each other or, even better, to their blogs.

A scant few actually dared to exhibit groupie-like behav-ior, including Delia Lambert (aka Morgan Carter's biggest fan). It was flattering at first, but one quickly tires of being fawned over 24/7, especially by an over-exuberant cheer-leader who has made it her mission in life to copy every sin-gle thing you do.

Finally, there were the haters, led by my very own neme-sis, Debbie Ackerman.

Debbie. *Ackerman*. I can't even write her name without

feeling my claws come out. She will pay for what she did to me—for spilling my secret to the entire world. I haven't figured out how exactly, but she. Will. *Pay*.

I'll have to bide my time, though. There's too much attention on me right now, and I'd get so totally busted exacting my revenge. Then wouldn't it look like sour grapes? Me, Morgan Carter, attacking a pudgy, pathetic nobody like Debbie Ackerman? It's . . . I don't know. Unseemly? I'm going to have to be very, very careful with this one—make sure I don't leave any tracks when the moment is finally right.

God, do I sound insane or what? Who cares about stupid Debbie Ackerman? Instead of cooking up half-brained revenge schemes, I *should* be trying to get to sleep. It's now going on 1 a.m. and I was hoping to get to school early tomorrow. I only have three more days to talk Ms. Janet Moore out of resigning from her job as school guidance counselor, and tomorrow's mission is going to require some serious physical stamina. Let's hope it works!

11/10

Operation "Save Ms. Janet Moore" has been aborted.

Why? Well, for one thing, it's become increasingly clear that Ms. Janet Moore doesn't want to be saved. All this time, I thought that she was leaving because of me—because I wigged out on her after my secret identity had been revealed.

I had assumed *she'd* been the one doing the revealing. And I was wrong—so wrong.

But it turns out that while Ms. Janet Moore *was* hurt

that I hadn't trusted her—or believed her when she said she'd kept my secrets in the strictest of confidence—her wanting to leave has absolutely nothing to do with me.

It does, however, have everything to do with a cushy new position as career counselor at a posh, all-girl boarding school in western Massachusetts.

"What if I promise to bring you M&M's every single school day from now until I graduate?" I asked, preying on her biggest weakness.

She shook her head and chuckled. "Sorry, Morgan, but candy doesn't make a very convincing counteroffer."

Turns out this boarding school offers free housing to its staff *and* a stipend for groceries and other expenses. This on top of a salary that Janet says is almost double what she's making at Snider. Plus, she'll be close enough to Amherst that she can take part-time classes if she wants.

"What kind of classes?" I demanded.

But she didn't answer. She just said, "I don't understand why you're so upset."

I couldn't figure out if she was genuinely clueless or if she was fishing for compliments—making me pay for my earlier transgressions.

Before Debbie Ackerman sold me out to the press, Janet and I were meeting in her office three mornings a week. She was the first person I'd ever confided in about what that sleazeball Harlan Darly did to me. And she was the first Fort Wayner outside of Trudy to know about my struggles with sobriety. Hell, she'd even been the one to tell me it was okay to make out with Eli Whitmarsh, regardless of what my Narcotics Anonymous sponsor thought about romantic relationships during the first year of recovery.

But before I could put any of that into actual words, Ms. Janet Moore leaned forward and patted my knee reassuringly. "I'll miss you too, you know. But you're going to be just fine, and you don't need me to tell you that."

"I suppose not," I agreed reluctantly.

She ripped a piece of paper off a mini yellow legal pad and scribbled down her new address and phone number. When she handed it to me, she said, "Promise me you'll keep in touch?"

So there you have it. No more Ms. Janet Moore. No more before-sunrise psych appointments, no more endless supplies of peanut M&M's.

Sigh.

Another sixty minutes until lunch—the highlight of my day. I don't mean that sarcastically, either. I mean that lately lunch is the only guaranteed time of the day when I get to see Eli.

When I was working on the Halloween Village fundraiser last month, Eli, Em, and I were practically together 24/7. But we were almost never alone. Now it's been a week since the village shut down, and I was sure this would mean Eli and I would have some actual quality time together. But between me fielding press requests and trying to stay on top of my studies and Eli's yearbook duties and his new obsession with a specialty camera he found at the Goodwill on Maplecrest a couple of weeks ago (a Helga or Holga or something he uses to do early-morning shoots, rendering him unable to give me rides to school), we haven't even had one hour together—let alone the time to go on an actual date. Yet.

Is it possible that Tater Tots have some hidden aphrodisiac quality that's yet to be discovered?

Yeah, didn't think so.

11/10—*Later*

So guess what? Turns out that Ms. Bowman, the woman they hired to replace Mr. Sappey, isn't just the new film studies teacher—she's also in charge of the drama program. How do I know this? Because Ms. Bowman cornered me after class today to ask if I had any intention of trying out for the spring musical. When I said no, she launched into this big speech about how great it would be for me to get involved.

"Just imagine," she said, a dreamy look in her eye, "how much you could teach the others!"

I told her I'd think about it, but my mind is made up. The answer is *no*. First of all, I can't commit to yet another activity. Thanks to Em, I'm still a Very Involved Panther, which means VIP meetings every other Wednesday afternoon (plus supplemental meetings when we're working on a big project like the Haunted Halloween Village fundraiser).

I still have my NarcAnon meetings every Thursday night to make sure I stay sober. Also, Trudy and I made a solemn pact to actually visit the gym three times a week—and yes, I'd like to leave a little bit of the time that's left open for a certain amateur photographer I know, whom I've grown quite fond of.

But besides all of that? I know the girls who'll be trying out for the play. Half of them are in my film class. And these are not girls who'd be okay with me, a onetime Oscar nominee, stealing the lead right out from under them.

Plus, LaTanya told me that Debbie Ackerman is a decent soprano and has landed fairly juicy parts in the last three musicals that Snider's put on. So, no. I don't see myself voluntarily joining a cast like that anytime soon.

Speaking of Debbie Ackerman . . . the bitch has gotten bold. It was bad enough when her pathetic social status was actually *elevated* by her role in my outing. But now it seems her confidence has been bolstered by a brand-new band of bimbo supporters.

Just a minute ago, in the lunch line, she actually approached me directly. *Directly.* I kid you not.

She walked right up to me and said, sweet as pie, "Have I told you that I like your new hair color, Morgan? It really thins out your face."

As if *she's* one to talk about chubby cheeks—I mean, the girl is shaped like a lawn troll!

But what really pissed me off—the thing that totally sent me over the edge—is the car. *Debbie's* car. The sporty, brand-new, silver Jetta GLS she purchased with some of the blood money she received for selling me out. (I say "some" because I know a good chunk of change went toward her two-hundred-dollar highlights, new wardrobe, and half the makeup from the Clinique counter at Marshall Fields.)

Where is *my* car? I want to know. Hell, I don't even have my license, and I'm seventeen!

Plus, last week I went to meet Eli in the yearbook room, and Debbie was actually draped over him like some kind of human pashmina. It's like, "Back off, slut! You can take my dignity, but you are *not* taking my man!"

Hmmm. Maybe I've been watching too much *Laguna Beach.*

My *Oprah* episode is set to air tomorrow, and to celebrate, Delia Lambert is throwing an *Oprah*-viewing party. At first I thought it was sort of sweet, but then I found out her mother is having it *catered*. While the Lamberts are far from poor, they aren't exactly the catered-party type either. At least, this is what Emily tells me. She also tells me that Delia's mom rented a large-screen projection TV that is so big, the delivery guys had to remove the bay window just to get it into the family room.

LaTanya got this photocopied invite that she said Meadow Forrester was passing out to their entire Spanish class, which is weird—I know for a fact that Delia can't stand Meadow Forrester, because Delia has told me six times now about how boobalicious Meadow hooked up with Delia's homecoming date under the bleachers last year before the dance was even *over*.

So now I'm stuck being the guest of honor at this overblown event I never asked for, when really I'd much rather be in my own living room with Trudy, Eli, and Emily.

Well, there's one consolation. Debbie Ackerman and her crew will *not* be in attendance, as Delia and the rest of the cheerleading squad have made it their mission in life to help me take Debbie down.

Sometimes it's good to have friends with pom-poms.

11/10—*Much later*

Eli surprised me as we were leaving the caf and asked me if I was free for dinner. I told him yes, even though Trudy and I were supposed to hit the Y to try out that new hot yoga class where the room temp hovers around eighty-five degrees. I figured Trudy would understand, seeing as I've been dying for me and E. to go on a real date, but then Eli said the invitation actually came from his *mother*.

"I don't get it," I said. "Why the formal request for my presence?"

Eli shrugged. "I think she just wants to get to know you better."

Sounded innocuous enough, right? Still, I felt suspicious. See, when I was Claudia, Mr. and Mrs. Whitmarsh were, like, totally in love with me. But then, after the outing, something changed. A big thing, actually.

First, Mr. Whitmarsh turned into this frat-guy dad, visibly pleased that it was *his* son who had snagged the starlet's heart. And then Mrs. Whitmarsh, who'd always seemed so genuine, started talking to me with a tight, practiced smile on her face—the kind people give you when they don't actually like you but are too mannered to say so.

"But your mother hates me," I practically whined.

"No, she doesn't," Eli said, for what must've been the hundredth time. "Besides, you have to come over. I want to show you the new prints I've been working on."

I called Trudy to postpone our gym date. She actually sounded relieved—like there was some other way *she* wanted to spend her evening too. (Most likely with Dave, her hot-'n'-heavy honey.)

My feelings might've been hurt—if I hadn't reminded myself I was the one to ditch her for a dude first.

Then it turned out that Emily had to stay after school—some student council meeting about a lack of fundage for the upcoming Winter Wonderdance—so Eli and I were actually alone for the first time in I don't know how long.

In the car, I asked, "Is your mom expecting us right away?"

Eli shook his head. "Why? Want to make a Munchies run?"

"Actually," I said slyly, "I *am* craving a little something— but not food."

"What? Starbucks?" Eli offered.

I batted my eyelashes a bit and said, "What do you think?" in my most suggestive tone.

I was rewarded with a blank stare.

I ran the tip of my tongue over my top lip, hoping that would help Eli get the message. It was something a director had me do once. According to Marissa, it made half the men in the crew pant.

Not so young Eli. All he said was, "You need some Chapstick?" and offered me a cherry-flavored tube.

"Oh, for Christ's sake!" I said, swatting the lip balm away. "Playing coy with you is like . . . like trying to teach Hilary Duff how to use eyeliner!"

"Relax," E. said with a grin. "I was thinking we could go somewhere private too. But I had to give you a hard time. Don't want you to think I'm easy."

I laughed, and Eli turned down a leafy little lane some-where between the seminary school and the golf course.

He turned off the ignition and pulled me to him, kissing me softly at first and then, gradually, with a little more urgency. It was so nice I almost didn't notice the parking brake digging into my side.

But then the inevitable happened—

Flashbulbs popping on all four sides of the car. There must've been a dozen or so photographers swarming all around us. One guy was so gutsy, he'd shimmied up the

13

front of the Camry, pressing his lens against the windshield while sprawling across the hood.

My cheeks grew hot; this was the first time the paparazzi had caught me and Eli in a "compromising position."

"Sam's going to kill me," I murmured, pulling a pair of oversized shades from my purse and slipping them over my eyes.

Eli, visibly shaken, rolled down his window. "Step away from the car, gentlemen, or I swear to God, I'll run you over."

This was not much of a deterrent, and I knew why. Sam had called me a couple of weeks ago to tell me the tabloids were offering between ten and twenty thousand for a clear shot of me snogging Eli (or, as the press had dubbed him, my "Midwestern Boy Toy"). He thought it was fabulous—Sam, I mean—and made me promise to hold off getting photographed with E. until he'd given the go-ahead. As much as I loved Sam, his pure glee at the possibility of capitalizing on my relationship with Eli made me feel a little uneasy.

Eli's face reddened as the hacks continued to shoot and call out things like, "Kiss her again!" and, "Come on, give us a little tongue!" The redder his face got, the more I knew his sweet-tempered nature was being stretched thin.

"Just start the car," I advised. "If you give it a little gas, they'll lay off."

Sure enough, when Eli revved the engine, the hacks backed away—all except Belly Boy, that is, who was still lying flat on the hood of the car.

Now I was getting pissed. It was bad enough that these jerks harassed me, but now they were messing with my man?

I rolled down my window. "Excuse me," I said, "I think

you got what you needed. Now please get off the car before we call the cops."

Belly Boy didn't move. In fact, I heard him say, "Oh, that's good. Keep it coming, honey—you look hot when you're angry."

I rolled up the window and turned to Eli. "Throw the car in reverse. He'll skid right off."

"Won't that hurt him?" Eli asked.

"Do you even care?"

But of course Eli cared, because he was still new to this whole "invasion of privacy" game.

So I tried to think of what Marissa would do in a situation like this. The idea came to me instantly and made me grin. I told Eli to close his eyes and keep them that way until I said it was okay. Then I rolled my window down again and leaned my torso out.

"Hey, slimeball. Over here."

I pulled my sweater up far enough to give Belly Boy a generous view of my black lace demi-cup bra. It had the desired effect; to get a proper shot, Belly Boy had to swing the lower half of his body to the right. In his excitement, he overshot his mark and slid right off the car onto the tar of the parking lot.

"Hit it!" I called to Eli, pulling my sweater back down and buckling myself into the passenger seat. "Open your eyes now and drive!"

Belly Boy was struggling to his feet just as E. peeled away.

"What did you do?" Eli asked when we were headed down the road.

"Ummm . . . nothing?" I said.

"Morgan." Eli's voice sounded stern. "What did you *do*?"

I sighed. "I flashed him, okay? But don't worry. He was too stunned to get the shot."

Eli's jaw tightened; I could see he wasn't pleased with my performance.

"Don't worry about it," I assured him. "Marissa and I used to do stuff like that all of the time. It's a . . . a defense technique."

He nodded silently.

"Come on, Eli," I said. "Don't let this ruin our afternoon, okay?"

After a pause, Eli's jaw relaxed. "Yeah, okay," he said. "Let's pretend the whole thing never happened."

It was a good plan. The problem was, after we turned onto the main road, we found ourselves followed by at least three more hacks. We tried to lose them, but to no avail. Eventually, we just gave up and headed over to the Whitmarshes'.

When we got to the house, Eli ran up to his room and got a set of the prints he'd been working on with his new camera. He'd tried several times to explain to me how the camera worked, but I didn't get it until I saw these new pictures. My favorite was a sharp-focus vignette of some bare black tree branches coated in a sparkling, clear glaze of ice. The background was a super-soft blanket of diffused light— you know, kind of how Barbara Walters's face looks during her annual pre-Oscar special.

"Oh, Eli," I said. "These are beautiful."

He beamed and then launched into a long explanation of how he'd set up each shot and how hard it had been to catch the light in just the right way.

Those pictures were another reminder of why I like Eli

Whitmarsh so much. I mean, how could you not fall for a boy who sees beauty where most people don't even bother to look?

Take me, for example. Eli started crushing on me as mousy Claudia long before he found out who I really was. Unlike half the male population of Snider High, who suddenly became very interested in the same girl who, in the eight weeks prior, had been totally invisible to them.

Eli didn't like me any *more* when he found out who I was, either. If anything, he was hurt that I'd lied to him about my past—a stage that, thankfully, we've been able to put behind us. I think.

Eli and I managed to sneak in a few kitchen kisses before Emily got home, though she did walk in on us leaning in for another.

"Hey! Get a room," she joked, poking me in the side.

Here's the great thing about dating your best friend's brother: you actually like it when she's around. I mean, there are three of us, right? And we all have our own special relationships with each other—me and Em, me and E., E. and Em. But we also work as a unit. So it wasn't like I was annoyed that Emily ended our umpteenth attempt at kissy face.

After a snack, the three of us went into the den for a little TV action but couldn't agree on what to watch. I wanted VH1's *Best Week Ever*. Eli wanted some *Quantum Leap* marathon on the Sci-Fi Channel, and Em wanted to catch *Chasing Amy* on one of the Encores.

But I put the kibosh on that one—quickly.

"No way!" I said. "I can't stand to watch Joey Lauren Adams in anything. She's like the poor man's Renée Zellweger, only way more annoying."

Emily and Eli gave me these blank stares, so I continued.

"You know what I mean, right? The poor man's thing? How they look sort of alike but one has talent and the other is . . . Joey Lauren Adams?"

More blank stares.

"Come on, you guys," I said. "Don't tell me you've never played this game before. Marissa and I used to do it, like, all the time."

"Is this like Who Would Win in a Fight?" Eli asked.

"*No*," I said, slightly offended. "That game jumped the shark after MTV did *Celebrity Death Match*."

"Jumped the wha?" Eli asked.

"Morgan," Emily said, laughing. "We have, like, zero idea what you're talking about. Translate, please."

"I can't really explain it. I'll have to show you," I told them. I trolled my brain for a good example. "Okay, how about this—Erica Christensen is the poor man's Julia Stiles."

"Who's Erica Christensen?" Emily asked.

I rolled my eyes. "You know—the druggie daughter from *Traffic*? The crazy psycho stalker from *Swimfan*?"

When I got no response, I said, "You guys know who Julia Stiles is. Right? *Ten Things I Hate About You? Save the Last Dance? Mona Lisa Smile?*"

"Sorry." Eli shrugged.

On the one hand, it was refreshing to be close to people who were totally removed from the business I'd grown up in. On the other, it was a little annoying that they couldn't speak the only language in which I was truly fluent (barring Spanish, that is. And French. But you know what I mean).

"Okay, okay," I said finally. "I've got it. The perfect example. But after this, you have to try. Person with the best example gets the remote, okay?"

The twins nodded—almost in unison.

"You've seen *Star Wars*, right?" I asked. "The original three?"

They nodded again.

"And *Rocky*—you have to have seen *Rocky*."

More nods.

"Okay," I said, grinning. "Carl Weathers is the poor man's Billy Dee Williams."

Eli goes, "Who is the what?"

"Stay with me now," I said, patiently. "Apollo Creed is the poor man's Lando Calrissian."

"Oh!" It was like a light had blinked on in Em's head. "I get it now."

But Eli frowned. "No way. Because Apollo Creed was, like, way cooler than Lando Calrissian."

"What?" I practically screeched. "How do you figure?"

"Because," Eli explained, "Lando needed that blaster gun. Apollo fought with his fists. And besides, didn't Lando betray Han Solo?"

"Yeah, but he made things right in the end," I argued.

"Still," Eli said, folding his arms. "I stand by my assessment."

"But Billy Dee Williams is the bomb!" I protested, jumping up off the couch. "Haven't you ever seen *Mahogany*?" I cleared my throat, steeled my eyes, and did my Billy Dee impression. "'Success is nothing without someone you love to share it with.'"

There was a pause. Then Emily and Eli cracked up at the exact same time.

I narrowed my eyes in mock annoyance. "Are you *laughing at me*?" I swatted each of them with a throw pillow.

"*With* you," Emily corrected, holding up her hands in defense. "We're laughing *with* you."

I plopped back down on the couch in a huff. "Fine," I said. "Watch your stupid *Chasing Amy*. I give up."

"No," Eli said. "Wait. How about this one? Vince Vaughn is the poor man's Vincent D'Onofrio."

"Please," I said. "Neither of them is the poor man's *anything*."

"Yeah, E.," Em agreed. "They're both hot, just in different ways."

Now it was Eli's turn to roll his eyes. "Fine. What about that guy from *Sweet Home Alabama*? The husband dude?"

"Josh Lucas?" I challenged. "What about him?"

"Is he the poor man's Matthew McConaughey?"

I grinned. "Nicely played, my boy. Nicely played."

So Eli got possession of the remote. We watched an episode of *Quantum Leap* where Sam had to "make right what once went wrong" or else someone would die—which is pretty much the plot of every episode of *Quantum Leap*.

Then, as the credits rolled, Em blurted, "Haley Duff is the poor man's Hilary Duff!"

I shook my head. "Doesn't count—they're related. Like, you couldn't say Mary-Kate is the poor man's Ashley. It doesn't work that way."

Her face fell for a second. Then she said, "Who's the blonde from *Scary Movie*?"

"You mean Anna Faris?" I asked.

Emily nodded eagerly and yelled out, "Anna Faris is the poor man's Cameron Diaz!"

"Good one!" I said, clapping. Eli gave her the remote and we ended up watching the last forty minutes of this Lifetime Movie *She's Too Young*, in which a good girl gets busy with a guy who gives syphilis to the entire high school. (Must TiVo movie for future viewing with Trudy.)

• • •

This went on until dinner, which is when the fun came screeching to a halt. Mostly because Mrs. Whitmarsh was making me very, very nervous.

She was trying to act all friendly, like she wanted to be my pal, but she wouldn't take her eyes off me the whole time. Like, I'm trying to chew on some green beans and she's staring at me. I take a sip of water, and she continues to stare. Finally, I asked her if I had something on my face and she said, "Oh, no. No." And then gave me one of her strained smiles.

I tried to ask her about her work—was accounting busy this time of year? She said not really and then started talking about one of her many volunteer gigs—specifically the one in which she works with women trying to kick drug addictions.

"Are you still attending meetings, Morgan?" she asked.

Emily yelped, "Mother!" and Eli turned bright red.

I didn't lose my cool, though. I simply said yes, that I was still going to NA on Thursday nights.

Mrs. Whitmarsh nodded and smiled. I could almost read the cartoon bubble over her head. *Good doggie*, it said. *Gooood doggie.*

After I helped clear the table and offered to do the dishes—"That's okay, Morgan," Mrs. W. said. "It's getting late and your aunt is expecting you home now. *Isn't she?*"—I got out of there quickly.

In the car, I asked Eli why his mother was being so weird around me, and instead of saying something reassuring like, "Oh, she must've had a busy day," or, "Don't worry, she's got a lot on her mind right now," he told me the stark truth: "She doesn't trust you."

"Trust me?" I said. "What does she think I'm doing? Lifting the silverware from the china cabinet?"

"Not exactly. More like . . . well, you know she works with addicts. She's had some rough experiences. Those women have to work for her trust. Prove that they're not going to lie or backslide or whatever. She's seen it too many times, so—"

"So I'm guilty until proven innocent," I said softly.

"I'm sorry," he said. "I know it's rough right now. But give it time. She'll like you again, I promise."

Although I appreciate that Eli's an honest person, I wish he would work on his delivery.

As if I hadn't felt uncomfortable enough around his mom.

Must go wash face and then hit the sack. Trudy's dropping me off early at school so I can see Ms. Janet Moore before homeroom.

11/11

When I got to Ms. Janet Moore's office this morning, she was boxing up the last of her personal belongings. The snot-yellow walls were bare, and so was the top of her beat-up metal desk. Even the crocheted blanket she'd artfully draped over her uncomfortable guest chair had been packed away. It was beyond depressing.

She seemed surprised to see me, and when I asked her why, she said, "I thought we did the goodbye thing."

It sort of stung, because here I am, agonizing over her impending departure and there she is, counting the number of seconds until she never has to see me again. So I mumbled something about Delia's *Oprah* party and how it would be nice if she'd be there, and she said she wished she could, but she still had a lot of packing to do.

Which just goes to show you: even the adults who seem to take a genuine interest in your happiness and/or well-being stop giving a shit once they're off the payroll.

I don't know why I ever thought differently.

God, I need chocolate.

11/11—*Later*

We needed to get to Delia's before 3 p.m., so there was no time to make a Starbucks pit stop to feed my caffeine addiction. I muttered something about hoping the Lamberts (or their caterer) would have some coffee available for consumption, and Eli said that if they didn't, he'd personally run out for a grande Sumatra.

How Eli understands my java love is a truly beautiful thing.

When we got to Delia's, I felt a lump form in my throat. There was no place to park. Literally *no place*. The street and front lawn were covered in cars—and the extra-large catering truck took up nine-tenths of the driveway.

This wasn't like working the Haunted Village, where I could hide behind a booth, signing autographs from a safe distance, feeling good about the fact that we were raising money for the children's hospital.

No, here it would be different. I'd have zero personal space—and the members of Mrs. Lambert's Red Hat Society were sure to be all over me.

In my former life, I would have popped a Klonopin to deal with the panic attack. Either that or downed a few shots of tequila.

Now? No such luck.

So there I was, in the twins' car, idling outside the Lamberts' house, feeling my chest tighten and my pulse speed up. I must've been wearing some of that anxiety on my face, because Eli said, "We don't have to go if you don't want to."

Em leaned in from the backseat, put a hand on my shoulder, and squeezed. "Just drop me off. I'll tell them you were sick or something."

I let out a breath. These were, clearly, the greatest friends in the universe.

But there was no way I could ditch the party. I mean, Mrs. Lambert had hired a *caterer*! I'd feel bad leaving after all the time and money she'd put into it. And after all, *she* didn't know how uncomfortable all of the hoopla would make me.

I took another deep breath, exhaled, and asked Eli if he thought he could fit the Camry on the small wedge of grass at the edge of the lawn. He did, then the three of us headed for the house—Emily in the lead and Eli slightly behind, guiding my elbow in that safe, comforting way he has.

Inside the house, it was worse than I'd imagined.

Within ten seconds, the oversized living-slash-dining room erupted in applause. For *me*. There were so many faces I couldn't tell them apart, although I was fairly certain I didn't know anyone there over the age of eighteen.

Trudy and her boyfriend were supposed to be in attendance, but I couldn't see her or Dave anywhere in the crowd. Hell, I could barely see the sixty-inch projection TV!

Not that it mattered.

A second later, the *only* thing in my scope of vision was Mrs. Lambert's ample bosom as she pressed me to her in a viselike hug. "Morgan Carter, we are so honored to have you here. Thank you for sharing this special day with my family and our friends."

Special day? She made it sound like I was getting married

or accepting a major humanitarian award—not pimping myself on a talk show.

One of the *classier* talk shows, granted, but still.

Before I could comprehend what was happening, Mrs. Lambert lifted two long-stemmed champagne glasses from a tray, handed one to me, and said, "Let's have a toast!"

I froze. Oh my God. *Who the hell gives a recovering alcoholic a champagne glass for a toast?*

I didn't hear Mrs. Lambert's words. I could only stare at the glass, that's how paralyzed I was. I couldn't drink the champagne. I knew I couldn't. But . . . wouldn't it be rude not to? But how could I, with everyone there, everyone watching my every single move? What would they think? What would *I* think?

Finally, Mrs. Lambert said, "Brava," and raised the glass to her mouth.

I froze. Everyone stared at me. Waiting to see what I'd do.

That's when Eli, stud that he is, snatched the glass from my hand and splashed the contents over the top of my head.

"Yay, Morgan!" He cheered like the champagne was Gatorade and I'd just scored the winning touchdown. "You rule!"

Horror screamed from Mrs. Lambert's face, but I knew immediately why Eli had done it. I'd told him about the time Marissa took me to Chicago and I almost—*almost*—downed a flute of bubbly.

His rescue attempt definitely lacked grace (my head? He couldn't think of anything to do with it except *pour it on my head?*), but I couldn't have been more grateful for his quick thinking—even if I *was* drenched in sticky sweetness.

Delia, meanwhile, flipped out. She ran over to Eli, punched his arm, hard, and yelled, "It was sparkling cider, you moron!" Then she hit him again. And again.

He didn't try to stop her, though, because he was too busy giving me this goofy grin.

All I could do was laugh. Loudly. The kind of laugh that makes your stomach muscles hurt because you're laughing so damned hard.

At first, Delia looked confused to see me laughing, but since she can't stop copying me for more than five minutes, soon she was laughing too.

It wasn't long before the whole room erupted, and I thought, *Maybe this party won't be DOA after all.*

And it wasn't, not really. Mrs. Lambert gave me a fluffy turquoise bath towel to dry off with, and Eli fixed me a plate of the catered goodies, including three miniature éclairs. (My favorite. Mrs. Lambert really did her homework!)

Trudy and Dave showed about a minute and a half before the show started, which gave me just enough time to explain why I reeked of apple cider. And then the *Oprah* theme song started to play, and everyone—even normally reserved Emily—shrieked.

A battalion of butterflies exploded in my stomach as Oprah turned to the camera and began—

"Today's guest, once dubbed America's Favorite Daughter, shocked the nation last year after an accidental overdose of drugs and alcohol almost claimed her life. Then, last month, she shocked the nation again when it was revealed that she had not only successfully completed a stint in rehab but was also hiding out in the Midwest, posing as an average American high school student."

Then Oprah shifted into her homegirl voice and

asked, "Y'all know who I'm talkin' about, right?"

Her middle-aged audience replied by screaming and clapping and whistling. For a moment, I was afraid their heads would pop off—just like in that old *SNL* sketch.

Oprah reverted to her "serious" voice and said, "Please welcome—*Morgan Car*ter."

More screaming and clapping. The camera pulled in tight on me entering from stage right.

It was surreal, seeing myself on-screen for the first time in more than a year. I'd chosen to wear a pearl gray suit over a pale blue silk shirt. The skirt had the tiniest little line of pleats at the hem. The jacket had the same pleats at the cuffs. My red hair had been coiffed into a 1940s movie star wave. A few false lashes in the corners of each eye and a smear of Chanel's Metal Garnet across my mouth completed the look, but it didn't hide my shy nervousness. Or—my God!—the twenty pounds I'd gained since that night outside the Viper Room.

Good thing I'd chosen Oprah over Katie. If anyone would forgive weight fluctuation, it would be Oprah's audience.

The first segment was totally awkward; I kept blinking and giggling at inappropriate moments. It was pathetic! I used to fly through interviews like this on automatic pilot, sometimes so stoned I wouldn't remember a single thing I'd said afterward.

But I always came off like a pro. Now I just seemed like an idiot teenager playing dress-up in her mama's closet.

And speaking of, Mama Bianca popped on-screen. Her outfit—a slate blue pencil skirt, black mules, and a black cashmere twin set draped with a Wilma Flintstone-sized strand of freshwater pearls—looked absolutely perfect on video and one hundred percent appropriate for the "mother of the recovering addict." If there's one thing my mother knows how to do, it's dress. And thanks to the magic of Botox and microdermabrasion, she looked like she had me when she was ten instead of twenty-four. In fact, my guess is that by the time I turn twenty-four, I'll be looking older than she will.

The Lamberts' house was pin-drop silent whenever the show was on, but during the commercial breaks, it got so loud my ears rang like church bells. Okay, okay—that's a bit of an exaggeration. But it was super-loud.

Eli sat next to me the entire time, and I squeezed his hand so tightly that neither one of us had circulation in our fingers for the duration of the episode.

I can't explain what I was feeling, exactly. Overwhelmed, maybe? After all, it had been so long. Even before I OD'd outside the Viper Room, my status as America's Favorite Daughter had been way in decline. Then after rehab, hiding out in the Fort and avoiding most of the media even after Debbie Ackerman outed me, I guess I didn't know how to respond to all the attention. It was no longer routine, and I wasn't even sure it was welcome.

I did Oprah's show because I had to tell my story somewhere (and I've always liked Oprah's Angel Network and all that). But I wasn't all, "Yay, I'm on *Oprah*!" It was more like, "If I have to do this, at least it's on *Oprah*."

Anyway, when we got to the segment where Oprah played me the taped messages from the other child stars, I got seriously choked up. Especially since they'd added some new ones between the taping and now. Like one from Robert Downey Jr. (who once offered to be my sponsor and who I adore in an "if you were twenty years younger I'd take you to my senior prom" kind of way).

Then, right before the commercial break, Oprah said, "Coming up next: Morgan's new best friends give us a tour of her life in Fort Wayne."

!

!!

!!!

So get this: while I was in Chicago, wishing the twins were there with me, they were in Fort Wayne with an *Oprah* film crew.

"They wanted to shoot it before you went to Chicago," Emily explained, "so they could show you the footage during the taping. But there was this whole big mess with scheduling and getting Mom to sign the releases for us, so . . ."

My head whipped back and forth between Eli and Em. E. was blushing furiously, but Emily just grinned and said, "You're going to love this."

It was a fun segment, shot in that faux-zany way where people look like they're walking twice as fast as they actually are. Emily did most of the talking, but Eli had a couple of big moments too—one of which consisted of him showing the camera some of the portraits he'd taken of me back when I was still Claudia Miller.

Finally, the two of them sat down—with a line producer, I'm guessing—to talk about, well, *me*. Oprah's voice narrated the conversation, the high point of which was this:

OPRAH: But geometry quizzes and slumber parties weren't the only things occupying "Claudia Miller's" thoughts. Just like any other seventeen-year-old girl, she got a crush . . . on a boy.
ELI (face reddened): I don't know if I could call her my girlfriend. . . .
EMILY: Oh, please. She *so* is.

[Audience at Harpo Studios laughs.]

ELI (even redder): We haven't, you know, officially talked about it or anything. But yeah. You know. She's . . . uh . . . special.

Hearing Eli Whitmarsh declare his affection for me to the entire *Oprah*-viewing audience was . . . *amazing*. Next thing I knew, I was grabbing his face and kissing him—*really* kissing him—right there in Delia Lambert's living room. Everyone did the "ooh" thing, just like studio audiences do when two of their favorite TV characters start spontaneously making out. Eli's and my kiss broke, and his face turned the color of sushi-grade salmon. I suddenly felt shy, too, and buried my face in Eli's shoulder to cover the blush creeping up my cheeks.

Then Oprah's voice interrupted the mood:

"Starlet or student?" she asked. "After the break, we'll find out what's next for Morgan Carter."

Eli gave me a look that I could only describe as quizzical.

"I need to tell you something," I whispered to him, but it was too loud in the room and he couldn't hear me. I tried again, but he kept shaking his head. So unless I wanted the entire room to hear what I had to say, I knew I'd have to keep quiet and wait for Eli to find out for himself.

The show returned. I closed my eyes. Heard Oprah asking me what my future held. Heard me saying, "Um . . . I don't know, really. I . . . uh . . ."

"Do you think you'll stay in Fort Wayne?" Oprah said. "Finish up high school? What about college?"

"I'd like to finish high school—" I said.

But Bianca cut me off. "Morgan will finish her junior year in Fort Wayne. After that, she'll be coming home. The only reason Morgan moved to Indiana in the first place was to help her recovery. Plus, I know she's eager to get back to work."

I could feel Eli's grip tighten on my hand. I kept my eyes shut, but I knew the camera was cutting to my reaction to Bianca's dropped bomb.

"Is that true?" Oprah asked. "Do you feel ready to resume your career?"

"I would like to work again," I said, slowly. "But I haven't really, you know, thought about it."

During the taping, I looked at Bianca and saw the supportive-mother smile on her face tighten, her eyes flash at me in the way only I could recognize. She was trying to intimidate me, but her actions had the opposite effect. Suddenly, my voice grew stronger, more certain.

"Sometimes I miss L.A.," I said to Oprah. "But mostly I'm enjoying Fort Wayne. Enjoying the chance to be a kid. I have my whole life to work. Right now, I'm happy just being me."

Oprah's studio audience applauded these words, and Bianca had to find her "I'm so proud of this kid" smile that she used to reserve for magazine shoots and prime-time interviews. But what startled me was that the people crammed into Delia Lambert's house started clapping, too, and shouting, "Yeah!" and stuff.

Except for Eli, that is. The corners of his mouth were turned up in a smile, but his eyes told a different story entirely. They were questioning me, trying to figure out whose answer was more honest: Bianca's or mine.

When the credits rolled, and some of the hoopla died down, I pulled Eli into the hallway and said, "I want you to know that I'm not going anywhere."

"Yet," he said.

I nodded. "You're right. I'm not going to spend the rest of

my life in Fort Wayne. But I really would like to finish out high school at Snider. And I really am thinking about going to college."

"What about your mother?" he asked. "Sam?"

"I've thought about it a lot," I told him. "And there are ways for me to work without having to drop out of school. Marissa and I knew some girls who didn't work as much as we did. They went to school most of the year, but if they got a job, they'd make arrangements with their teachers to keep up with the work while they were absent."

He listened intently, but I could still see the worry knitted into his eyebrows.

"Look," I said finally. "I've got seven months to deal with Bianca. This might not even be an issue by then. So let's just enjoy ourselves, okay?"

Finally, I got a genuine smile out of Eli. He kissed my temple and said, "Yeah, okay. You're right. Let's go have some fun."

In the end, Ms. Janet Moore never showed up, but I realized it didn't matter. She might have blown me off, but hey—I was surrounded by good people who honestly cared about me, like Trudy, Emily, and even the Lamberts.

And, of course, Eli. Eli Whitmarsh, my sweet, sensitive, understanding boyfriend.

Me! With an actual boyfriend!

Take that, Debbie Ackerman. You may have gotten the Jetta, but I ended up with the boy.

I think I'll end on that note. It's almost midnight, and I've been writing in this journal for close to three hours. No wonder I never get any sleep!

11/11—*Five minutes later*

Ms. Janet Moore just called here. At 11:57 p.m. To ask me if I wouldn't mind coming to her office before homeroom tomorrow.

The nerve of that woman! Forget goodbye—I say, good riddance!

11/12

I take it back. The part about good riddance? There was a reason Ms. Janet Moore called me to her office today. And I'm really glad she did.

I got there maybe ten minutes before first bell, which was my passive-aggressive way of giving her the finger while still complying with her request. I turned my face into stone and put on my "I don't like you, I merely tolerate you" armor, because I'd sworn I wasn't going to let her know how hurt I was.

"Hey," she said in a soft voice as she spotted me in the doorway. "You showed."

"You needed something?" I shot back.

She nodded. "I wanted to give you this." Janet took my left hand and pressed something into my palm. When I saw what it was—her own five-year sobriety chip—my cool resolve melted clean away.

"Why?" I asked, tears springing into my eyes. "Why would you give this to me?"

"Because I'm proud of you," she said, smiling. "I watched the *Oprah* thing. You were so poised, so articulate . . . and you know, you helped a lot of people yesterday. Just talking about how you overcame your addictions will inspire others to action."

"You watched?" I said, trying to blink back the tears. "I thought you had a lot of packing to do."

"I did," she conceded. "But that's not why I turned down your invite."

"Then why?"

"Because I knew how hard it would be to watch you tell your story. Especially since I knew it firsthand. I didn't want to start blubbering in a room full of students."

"Then why didn't you say that?" I cried. "I thought you didn't care."

Ms. Janet Moore shook her head. "Goodbyes are hard for me, Morgan. But don't think for a second that I don't care about you or what happens to you."

It was something I really needed to hear.

11/12—*Later*

So lunch today was weird. It was the first time I'd seen Eli since he and Emily dropped me off at my Narcotics no-longer-Anonymous meeting yesterday after the party.

Eli seemed all extra shy and awkward. Plus, he looked really tired, like maybe he hadn't slept last night. I tried to ask him if everything was okay, but he just said, "Uh, yeah," and jammed some cafeteria mac 'n' cheese down his throat.

Later, I cornered Emily and asked her what she knew. She sighed and said, "My mom watched the *Oprah* show too."

"So?" I asked.

"*So*," she told me, "she was concerned about what Eli said."

"About me," I amended. "What Eli said about *me*."

Em nodded. "Right. Not to mention what your mother said."

"About me leaving at the end of the year?" I asked.

She nodded again.

Well, that would explain it.

Mrs. Whitmarsh officially hates me. What I couldn't understand, though, was how she could devote so much of her time to helping recovering addicts and still disapprove of her son dating one.

Okay. Maybe I *do* get it.

But she could at least honestly get to know the real me before actively hating me! And despite what Eli said about dinner the other night—about how his mom did want to get to know me—it was clear that what she really wanted was to keep an eye on me.

Back to Emily.

"Cut him some slack, Morgan," she said. "He's never actually rebelled against our parents before. It was different when he was with Sarah, because our moms had been sorority sisters in college and they were, like, *hoping* she and E. would hook up."

I winced. Sarah. The infamous ex-who-moved-to-Texas-and-took-Eli's-heart-with-her Sarah.

"You could've warned me," I said. "We passed notes all through English—literally minutes before lunch! You didn't mention your mom's reaction *or* Eli's weirdness even once!"

Em frowned. "I don't want to have to 'warn' you," she said. She shifted her book bag higher up on her shoulder. "Listen—I think it's cool you're dating my brother and all, but I don't want to, like, be a third member of the relationship. Okay?"

I blinked. I hadn't thought about it in those terms before. I mean, the three of us hung out together all the time and it never felt awkward or uncomfortable. But if I was going to be Eli's girlfriend . . . well, I guess it did change the dynamic.

If Em had a boyfriend in high school, things would be so

much easier. We'd be a regular foursome, instead of a three-some with guest appearances by Caspar, Em's hottie boyfriend who's a college freshman at IPFW.

Though I guess I shouldn't complain. I've only met Caspar a couple of times, but he's way smart and totally sweet on Emily. Plus, he's got this wacky sense of humor and is always telling these hilarious "Why did the chicken cross the road?" jokes. (Example: "Why did the chicken cross the road? To get some crack. Why did the chicken cross the road again? To get his daddy some crack." Okay, maybe you had to be there, but trust me—hilarious.)

Anyway, considering Emily's last love interest was that awful hypocrite Joey Harkus, it's about time she landed a guy who makes her feel good about herself.

Kind of like Eli does for me.

11/12—Much later

After school, the twins and I decided to make a Munchies run and get some Scooby Snacks (hot potato goodness!), but on our way out to the car, we were ambushed by Delia Lambert, clad in full cheerleading gear. "Hey guys!" she said, a little too brightly. "What's the haps?"

How very 1990s of her. I was about to point this out, but before I could get in one of my little digs, my cell phone started bleating the theme song to *Charlie's Angels*. It was Bianca, calling me in the middle of an appointment with her colorist Carré (pronounced Ca-RAY, not Carrie, as I have been chastised on more than one occasion).

"Can't talk long, darling," she said. "Ca-RAY wants to try this new paraffin foot dip on me. But I wanted you to know that I TiVo'd our *Oprah* episode yesterday and watched it this morning while I was on the elliptical. You were smashing, sweetheart! Smashing! Papa Sam thinks so too. Kisses!"

She hung up before I could even respond.

Several things about that phone call made me uneasy. First, why had Bianca TiVo'd the show instead of watching it as it aired? Very unlike her. Second, I do not understand why Bianca insists on referring to Sam as "Papa," especially since he has been my manager fifteen times longer than he's been her third husband and I've always, always called him Sam. *Just* Sam. Finally, Bianca only uses the "kiss and hang up" routine when something unpleasant is happening, like the time I lost out on the part of Dawn, Buffy the Vampire Slayer's younger sister, because I was twelve pounds too fat, though I later found out Joss Whedon had scripted the part for Michelle Tractenberg and I never stood a chance, but whatever. Or like the time my biological father was trying to blackmail Sam into giving him several thousands of my dollars by threatening to release some nudie pictures he had of my mom from when they first got married.

So I knew something must be up. Something big.

I immediately dialed Sam but got voice mail at each of the three numbers I tried (work, cell, home).

In between leaving suitably frantic messages—my biggest fear being that the pictures of me and Eli kissing had come out, and Sam was having a conniption trying to spin it—I caught snippets of the twins' conversation. Delia Lambert was getting herself invited on my Munchies run. Great.

Now, we all like Delia. She tries very hard to keep things positive. She's also got one of those faces that makes it very hard for you to say no to her. She looks like . . . like Jessica Simpson's puppy, only in human form. Like you could kick her hard and she'd still want to cover your face in kisses. So even though I would've preferred leaving Delia behind, it didn't feel like an option.

Emily wanted to drive, so I instinctively got in the back-seat, thinking Delia could sit up front and Eli and I could be alone in the back. But before you could say, "Mini Me," Delia hopped in next to me, sitting so close I couldn't figure out which seat-belt holder was hers and which was mine.

If only there was a polite way to say, "Back off, baby— you're stealing my oxygen."

Another thing about Delia is that she likes to talk. A lot. I tried to thank her again for the party but could barely get half a sentence out before she cut me off and started bab-bling something like, "Oh, don't even worry about it; it was our pleasure. I mean, to have the most important actress of our generation in our house and *blah blah blah* . . ."

It wasn't long until Delia's motormouth got around to asking me about the auditions for *Oklahoma!* Would I be there? And what was I going to wear? And did I have a song prepared? And did I prefer to sing to a backing track or would I do it a cappella?

"I'm not even sure I'm trying out," I interrupted her.

This made her shriek. Literally, shriek.

"But you have to try out!" she wailed. "You're supposed to be Laurey, and I'm going to be Annie! It will be perfect!"

I didn't know who she was talking about—characters from the musical, most likely—but finding out that Delia intended to be my cast mate was all the information I needed to make my final decision.

"It's my schedule," I explained. "Too many meetings, too many issues with geometry. Plus, I'm not much of a singer."

"But I told her you'd do it!" Delia cried. "Promised her, even."

"Who?" Emily and I asked at the same time.

Delia looked away. "Ms. Bowman. I told Ms. Bowman that I could get you to at least try out, and she said if you agreed to be in the play, I would be guaranteed a speaking role."

Unbelievable! And I thought Bianca had cornered the market on emotional blackmail.

Clearly, Delia had been taking notes.

"But why?" I asked her. "Why would you promise something you couldn't deliver?"

Delia sighed. "Because I really thought I could get you to do it. Especially after the rumors that Debbie Ackerman has been spreading about you."

"Wait!" Em commanded, pulling the Camry into the Munchies parking lot. "This is getting juicy, and I don't want to miss a *word*."

Once we were seated and had placed our order (Scooby Snacks all around!), Emily said, "Okay, so what's this about Debbie spreading rumors?"

Delia was more than happy to share the gossip she'd heard. Highlights included:

- Debbie telling Meadow Forrester that I'd never try out for the school play because I'm too stuck up to "mingle with the masses" (not true; I'm a VIP member, right? I'm just not sure I'm a midwestern theater brat);
- Debbie asking Lauren Johnson if she'd noticed me acting edgy lately, and did it look like my eyes were all bloodshot

from going on a bender? (*if* my eyes are at all red, it's from lack of sleep and/or too much caffeine and *nothing* else.);

- Debbie suggesting to Bethany Parker that I was so concerned about my post-rehab weight gain that I'd decided to try bulimia on for size (the part about the concern is sort of true, but the rest isn't—I cry every time I puke, because it hurts, and it's gross, and I can't imagine what's it's like for someone to feel compelled to do that four or five times a *day*).

There was more, but I'd rather not waste my time recounting it all. Suffice it to say: Debbie Ackerman doesn't want me trying out for *Oklahoma!*

And that, of course, is exactly why I'm going to do it.

11/12—*Much, much later*

To: Marissa Dahl
From: Morgan Carter
Subject: Drama queen finds Prince Charming in unlikeliest of places (?)

Dearest Marissa,

I'm not even sure if you'll have e-mail access—do they get high-speed Internet in the Russian tundra?—but I figure at the very least you'll get this when you return home. I CAN'T BELIEVE YOU'RE GOING TO BE IN THE NEXT JAMES BOND MOVIE. You are a BOND GIRL! You have ARRIVED!

Anyway . . .

While you're off solidifying your status as sex kitten of the year, I'm contemplating conquering the Snider High School drama club's production of *Oklahoma!* Okay, stop laughing. I don't have much choice—if I don't try out, then I run the risk of everyone thinking that I'm a total snob, like I think I'm too good to be in their little Podunk production. Of course, when I *do* try out, I will have to face the wrath of some *Mean Girl-*esque dyed blondies who already hate my guts for stealing their spotlight. Not to mention that beyotch Debbie Ackerman, who hates my guts for stealing "her" beloved Eli. But whatever.

Oh, and I was on *Oprah* yesterday. Yeah, a whole hour devoted mostly to me. I wish you could've been there. The whole time I was in Chicago I kept thinking of you and our impromptu trip earlier this fall. Remember how we saw Katie Holmes, and I was so scared she'd recognize me that I hid behind you like you were my human shield?

So the boy was on *Oprah* too, with Emily. Marissa, he told Oprah that I was "special"! Well, he told Oprah's camera crew, anyway. I have to tell you how awesome it was to hear him say that. And on national TV, no less!

I know what you're thinking: why does this common midwestern boy make me so damned happy? Well, for one thing, he's not common. Not at all. He's really, really brilliant, and he devotes a lot of his time to all these really good causes, and he takes amazing photographs of ice, and he can play the *Mission: Impossible* theme song on his theremin. And yeah, he's sort of geek-like, but in this super-cute, Seth-on-the-first-season-of-*The O.C.* kind of way—especially since I started styling his wardrobe.

But also: whenever he looks at me in that certain way—you know what way I'm talking about, right?—when he looks at me that way, I can't help but melt into a little pool of butter.

Yeah, I said it.

This kitten is beyond smitten.

My only concern—besides the fact that his mother sort

of hates me—is, what if Eli decides that dating a celebrity is too much work? Like Hugh Grant in *Notting Hill*? The other day the paparazzi caught us fooling around and this one dude scaled E.'s car and it totally freaked him out. I didn't have the heart to tell him that was minor compared to what I used to deal with in California.

I guess I can fall off that bridge when we come to it, right?

Stay warm—and say hi to my old friend Stoli for me. . . .

—M.

11/13

Tonight was a total disaster.

It was supposed to be me and Eli's first official double date with Emily and Caspar. But then Eli called and asked me if I'd mind if we went alone, and he said it in this throaty voice that was sort of hot. So of course I said fine.

But then it wasn't. Hot, I mean. Or fine. Because it turns out that Eli didn't want to get me alone so that he could cover my face with passionate kisses or make further declarations of his love. No, he wanted to get me alone so we could *talk*.

I didn't know this, of course. Not at first. Not when Eli suggested a romantic dinner for two at Casa d'Angelo.

(Actually, he said something like, "How about Casa's?"— I just assumed the romantic part.)

And at first everything was okay. I signed a few autographs; we split an order of the calamari; we joked about how boring we were because I ordered the vegetarian lasagna (my favorite) and he got the cannelloni (his favorite). We'd just decided to leave room for dessert when Eli busts out with this:

42

ELI: So you were right about my mom hating you.

ME: Is that some kind of joke?

ELI: Not exactly.

ME: Wait — *what*?

ELI: She didn't use the word *hate*. But she did suggest that I stop seeing you in a boy-girl kind of way.

ME:

ELI: She had some valid points, Morgan.

ME:

ELI: Like, I'm still getting to know you. The *real* you, I mean.

ME: But —

ELI: Yeah, I know. You were always the real you, except for the dyed hair and fake glasses and made-up background. Oh, and that sob story you stole from that Lifetime TV movie you were in, about how your psycho dad killed your dog Muppet and left him on your doorstep as a warning.

ME: Her. Muppet was a girl.

ELI: Morgan, *Muppet wasn't real!*

ME: How many times do I have to apologize for all of that? And you — *you* were the one who said people would understand —

ELI: Eventually. I said they'd understand eventually.

ME: So you're not there yet? To the understanding part? Is that what you're trying to tell me?

ELI: No.

ME: No, you're not there? Or no, that isn't what you're trying to tell me?

ELI: A little of both.

So then I didn't know what to say. I mean, it sounded like Eli had already made up his mind. Or let his mommy make up his mind for him. And the waiter was clearing our plates and asking us about dessert, and it was all I could do to keep from crying, and Eli—Eli calmly ordered two tiramisus, like he hadn't just rocked my carefully constructed Indiana world. He ordered me a cappuccino too, just like I would have for myself if I hadn't been holding back a torrent of anger and/or tears.

"You look upset," Eli remarked when the waiter left.

I chuckled bitterly. "You think?"

"All I'm saying is that maybe we should slow down a bit. Get to know each other better before anything is . . . official."

"Well, you're officially an asshole," I said through gritted teeth.

When he didn't respond, I continued. "Why don't you be a man and admit what this is really about? You can't stand disappointing your mother, and until she likes me, you're not allowed to either."

Eli took a sip of water and looked away. "It's not like that, Morgan."

"Oh, really?" I said, balling up my napkin and throwing it down on the table. "You're a good boy, Eli Whitmarsh. You don't know how to be anything but. Why don't you call me when you grow a pair, okay?"

Then I stormed out of the restaurant.

I expected Eli to follow me out, but when five minutes passed and there was no sign of him, I called Trudy on my cell to ask her to pick me up.

I cried the entire ride home.

Trudy asked me if I wanted her to have a talk with Mrs. Whitmarsh to see if she could smooth things out between us, but I said no. "It shouldn't matter if she likes me or not," I said between sniffles.

Trudy nodded. Then, after a long pause, she said, "I know this isn't what you want to hear, but maybe Eli is right."

"Don't tell me you're on his side," I said.

"No. But it's just . . . well . . . the poor kid's face is plastered on the front of every supermarket tabloid."

"What?" I practically shrieked. "Since when?"

Trudy gasped. "I thought you knew! Remember, you were explaining how you had to flash that guy to get him off Eli's car?"

"Yeah."

"Well, they got the picture of you and Eli." She paused. "They also got a picture of you . . . um, hiking your shirt up."

My eyes went wide. That lucky sonofa—

He must have gotten off a shot when he slid from the hood!

I didn't know the pictures had come out—in fact, I'd been trying to pretend it never happened. After all, I hadn't heard anything from Sam or Bianca or that idiot freelance publicist they hired to do some long-distance consulting from California.

Then I remembered how weird Bianca had been about *Oprah* and how I'd thought something was up. This, without a doubt, had to be that something.

No wonder Mrs. Whitmarsh was freaked!

"I should call Eli," I said, looking around for the cordless phone. "I bet that's why he's so spooked. I have to explain. I didn't even know!"

Trudy placed her hand gently on mine. "Don't call him, Morgan. Give him a little space. He'll come to you. When he's ready."

So now I have to sit here and wait.

And it's official. I have become *that* girl. The one who jumps every time the phone rings, hoping it's him.

Okay, so it's only been like four hours, but still.

Trudy and Dave were supposed to take Dave's son, Ryan, to a matinee at the Schouweiler Planetarium this afternoon, but when Tru saw how devastated I was that Eli had yet to phone, she called Dave to cancel. I told her not to—told her it would do me good to spend some time wallowing on my own—but she said, "Nonsense," and promptly booked us pedicures at Eden Spa & Salon.

God, I love this woman.

While our feet were soaking in lavender-scented whirlpool baths, Trudy asked me if I'd figured out how to handle the whole Eli thing at school tomorrow.

"Handle?" I said. "There's nothing to handle. He's not going to call, Trudy. We're over. Done. *Finito*."

"You don't know that," Trudy said. "It hasn't even been a full twenty-four hours."

I shook my head. I'd made up my mind about a few things when I couldn't sleep last night.

"It doesn't matter," I told her. "I don't care how 'spooked' he may or may not be—it was really not cool of him to ambush me like that at Casa's. You don't treat someone you care about like that, you know?"

Trudy said she could see where I was coming from but that she hoped I'd keep an open mind.

"Why should I?" I said. "*He* certainly hasn't. Not to mention his mother."

I know I sounded tough, but I figured that if I was the one who was angry, then at least I could feel in control.

So far, it was working. Kind of.

Trudy asked about Emily and how I thought my new attitude toward Eli would affect my friendship with her.

I didn't think that was going to be a problem. I felt no ill will toward Emily whatsoever. Then Trudy said, "Yes, but Morgan—they share a car. You all eat lunch together. It's not like you can spend time with her and avoid her brother."

I could feel the frown forming on my face. "Sure, I can. I'll get my own car. I'll eat lunch at another table. It's entirely doable."

"Except," she pointed out, "that you don't have a driver's license, and if you switch lunch tables, you then put Emily in the awkward position of having to choose between you and Eli."

"I don't like you today," I said, scowling. "Aren't you supposed to be cheering me up?"

Trudy reached over and patted my hand. "I know you're hurting, honey. All I'm trying to say is that you might want to reconsider your stance. Eli's been a good guy so far. And it's got to be scary to realize that the girl you're crushing on is actually an international superstar. . . ."

Here she struck a nerve—a pretty deep one.

See, since I started crushing on Eli, in the back of my head, I've always had this teensy little fear. I worried that one day Eli would find out the truth about me and then he'd realize it was Claudia he wanted to be with, not Morgan.

Right now, it seemed that—maybe—my fear was warranted after all.

A blond Glamazon came by and handed us each steaming bowls of rosewater tea, compliments of the house.

I shook myself out of my funk, cradled the bowl in my hands, and thanked her. I had taken several calming sips before she explained that we were supposed to use the steam to open our pores. (Tasted pretty good, though, before the Glamazon informed me of its true purpose.)

I nestled the bowl and its remaining liquid under my chin, closed my eyes, and had a good long think. If Marissa were here, she'd snap a wet towel at me and say, "Morgan Carter, I will *not* allow you to fall apart over some unworthy country boy who's too chickenshit to go for a great thing when she's staring him in the face." And then I'd get all flustered and try to explain to her that Eli isn't unworthy, or "country," or chickenshit. Then I'd tell her all the things about him that make me feel melty, like how he's always framing shots in his mind, whether he's got his camera or not, or how when he calls me late at night, instead of saying goodbye, he says, "Sweet dreams, you." At which point, she'd interrupt me with a sigh and say, "If you're going to get this defensive, then you obviously need to just go for it. Regardless of what I think."

So now I'm fighting with myself . . . on paper . . . and *losing*. There's something wrong with that, I think.

If Ms. Janet Moore hadn't abandoned me for boarding school, I could ask her about it tomorrow morning. Or if Emily wasn't Eli's loyal sister, I could call her and see what *she* thinks. And of course if Marissa wasn't in the Russian tundra, sans viable cell phone signal, I could have an actual conversation with her instead of the pathetic virtual one I just scripted in my journal.

God. I am so alone.

And I am *so* not looking forward to school tomorrow.

11/15

Something strange: when I went into my locker this morning, someone had stuck a folded cover of *Star* into the slats. The main picture was of me and Eli going at it in the Camry. We had been Photoshopped into a heart that was ripped down the middle.

The headline read, "Problems in Paradise for Podunk Princess?"

Now, who would want to be 100 percent certain that I saw that cover? I wondered. And who'd actually browse the tabs on a regular basis?

The only thing I could think—besides it being some random student I didn't know—was that this was the work of Debbie Ackerman. I imagined she was tickled, seeing how the tabloids were spinning this whole me-and-Eli thing. Hoping, if I know her (and I think I do), that their totally fake story would sound real enough to make Eli doubt me in a major way. Which in Debbie's mind would translate into her having a real shot of worming her way into Eli's fractured heart.

No question, I decided. This had Debbie Ackerman's fingerprints all over it.

So when I saw her skulking by my locker not a minute or two later—like she was on a recon mission or something—I balled up the tearsheet and tossed it at her. My aim was good: the paper ball bonked her square on the forehead.

"What was that for?" she yelled. As if she didn't know.

"You're wasting your time, you know," I told her. "Not just with Eli. I mean, the tabloids, Deb? I would've thought a smart girl like you would spend her time and money on something actually worth reading. Like maybe that South Beach diet book? You could really stand to beef up on your carb IQ." Then I cut my gaze to her tummy, which still mushroomed out from the too-tight waistband on her jeans.

Instead of turning red, as she would've just five short weeks ago, Deb reached out and pinched my side. "Looks like you've got more than an inch there yourself, Morgan. I'd think someone with your money could afford a little lipo—or, at the very least, a personal trainer."

And then *she* sauntered away from *me*. An actual saunter!

That girl has got to go down.

I just need to figure out how.

11/15—*Later*

Okay, so this is really weird: I'm in fourth-period English and *Emily isn't here.*

For those of you playing along at home, Emily, like, *never* misses school. Plus, she's so organized that if she has to leave early for a dentist appointment or whatever, she lets me know a week in advance and e-mails me a reminder (so I won't worry and so I can gather her assignments for her).

But even when she's not missing a class, Emily always, always calls on the weekend. Except this weekend, she didn't.

I realized this late last night, as I was agonizing over having to see Eli today and whether or not I was going to attempt contact with him or wait for him to come to me.

Suddenly, I was all, "Why hasn't Em called me? Is it because Eli told her what happened on our distastro-date Saturday night? Is she mad at me for walking out on him? Or has Mrs. Whitmarsh poisoned her too?"

Needless to say, I didn't get much sleep. I tried to conceal this fact by sporting a pair of blue-tinted "sunglasses" (knock-offs from Tarjay—decorative only), but Mrs. Chappelle said it was against dress code for me to wear them inside.

This is kind of a stupid rule, seeing as Dawna Myers, this total geek girl in my gym class, wears prescription glasses with clear plastic frames and the lenses tinted half blue (tops) and half pink (bottoms). You know, the sort of thing that was *trés chic* circa 1982?

But whatever. Now I have exactly sixteen minutes to figure out what to do about lunch. Because what if Emily isn't there, either? I really don't think I can deal with seeing Eli face-to-face without using Em as a buffer. And if I don't sit at my usual table, should I bother going to the cafeteria at all?

If I had my driver's license, I could do the cool-kid thing and head off campus for lunch, maybe take an extended period and hit up a Red Robin. But no. I don't have my license, I don't have a car, and I'm supposed to be avoiding red meat per Trudy's and my new wellness plan.

I guess I could sit with LaTanya. I mean, it's sort of

weird that we have the same lunch period yet never, ever sit together.

Granted, we went through a week or two of deep freeze on our friendship after Sam paid her off to keep quiet about who I was. But we've since reconciled, and she's even gone to Munchies with me and Em once or twice.

The problem is that LaTanya sits with the black kids.

Not that I have any problems with the black kids. In fact, I would go so far as to say that they're the only kids here who have any real sense of fashion. It's just that at Snider High, the white kids sit with the white kids and the black kids sit with the black kids. Sometimes the Latino girls will sit with the black boys, but the black girls (or boys, for that matter) aren't welcome at the Latino-only tables. There aren't enough Asians for them to have their own tables, so they mostly blend in with the white kids. Except the Asian girls are even more fashionable than the black girls—not including my evil lab partner, An-Yi—so they don't really "blend" so much as create mini-clusters of coolness and sophistication among the vanilla hordes.

It's all a little too *Do the Right Thing*, if you ask me.

11/15—*Even later*

I've made a new friend!

It's true. I was standing in the middle of the cafeteria, still debating whether or not to sit with Eli at my usual table or worm my way into LaTanya's crew, when this guy literally walks into me. I said, "Hey, watch where you're going, jackass!" and instead of getting smart with me or calling me on my bitchiness, he backs up, does this deep, theatrical bow, and says, "I apologize, milady. Your radiant beauty must've disarmed my depth perception."

I said, "Whatever," and was about to walk in the opposite direction when the guy straightened up and I got a full-on look at him.

Oh, *man*.

Imagine, if you will, the child that would result from throwing the genes of George Clooney, Paul Rudd, and Catherine Zeta-Jones into a petri dish and you *might* come close to the gorgeousness that was staring me in the face.

The gorgeousness of Riley Augustine.

(Yes, it's true—some of my Hollywood shallowness remains.)

Riley is the resident Snider heartthrob, and rumor has it he is a shameless flirt.

Hanging out with the twins, however, I've never really had the opportunity to test the theory. Riley moves in a totally different (read: much, much cooler) circle.

"*Hel*-lo," I said, blatantly giving him the up-down.

This did not escape Riley's notice. "Are you lost, little girl?" he asked. "Big Daddy would be more than happy to escort you to a table."

I said, "Did you just call me 'little girl'?"

"I did," he replied. Then, in an exaggerated whisper, he added, "Did it make you hot?"

Without missing a beat, I said, "Ooh, yeah, baby. If you give me your class ring, I'll let you feel me up in the janitor's closet."

He laughed—a deep, throaty laugh that made me smile in return.

53

"Maybe I should introduce myself first," he said. "I'm Riley. Riley Augustine."

We shook hands, and I said, "Hello, Riley-Riley Augustine."

"And you are . . . ?" he said.

I cocked my head. "I'm fairly certain you already know who I am."

"Sure," he said, snatching the basket of fries off my plate. "But I was hoping I could get to know you better."

It was adorable, this faux-punk attitude. And more than flattering, considering how in-the-basement my self-esteem had been lately. But I wasn't about to let *him* know that.

So I said, "Are your pickup lines always this cheesy?"

"That's my girl," he shot back. "Keep pretending you don't like me. It'll make the kissing even hotter."

So there we were, the two of us, standing in the middle of the cafeteria, and people were beginning to stare. I couldn't see Eli from my vantage point, but if he was in the room, I'd bet money that he was watching too.

"I think I'd like that escort now," I said.

Riley nodded. "Of course. I mean, not that you have a choice. I'm holding your fries hostage." He popped a handful of them into his mouth, then led me to a partially empty table not far from where I usually sat with the twins and Delia. I chose the side facing away from that table so that if Eli was watching, he'd only see my back.

My ass had barely hit the seat when Delia whooshed in and placed her lunch tray down next to me.

"There you are!" she said. "Why are we sitting over here today? Something going on between you and Eli?"

Now, I'm not cold enough to think of this "Riley Augustine" as an instant Eli replacement. But I certainly didn't appreciate Delia dropping his name into the conversation five minutes into my new friendship.

"I don't want to talk about it," I said.

"Why not?" Delia and Riley asked in unison.

I blinked twice.

"Excuse me," I said to Riley. "This is kind of a *private* conversation."

"Oh, okay," Riley said. "Just as long as you promise me that our privates can have their own conversation later."

He grinned, then bit into his sandwich.

When I didn't laugh—or respond at all, really—Riley said, "Okay, bad joke. Way, way over the line. You probably think I'm the world's biggest dick right now—"

"Don't flatter yourself," I said, cutting him off. "I'm guessing it's travel-sized."

I held up my pinkie finger and wiggled it around. It took Riley a couple of beats to get the joke. Then a slow smile spread across his face.

"Will you be my prom date?" he asked.

I laughed. "Let's just get through lunch first, shall we?"

Delia kept giving me these quizzical looks, like, "What is going on here?" but I ignored them. Harder to ignore was her now-daily harassment about whether or not I was trying out for the school play.

She took a deep breath, then started right in. "Debbie Ackerman is going around telling everyone that she's got the lead locked up—*no matter who auditions*," Delia informed me. "Can you believe it? The nerve? I can't wait until you get on that stage and blow her away."

Looking at me, Riley said, "Oh, so you're into theater?"

Delia, missing the sarcasm, turned her own raised-eyebrow

55

stare onto him. "Don't you know who you're talking to?"

Riley shrugged. "Should I?"

Delia's jaw dropped so wide open, I could have stuffed my entire sandwich into the void.

"I don't know, Delia," I said, re-focusing her attention. "It's complicated."

"How?" she demanded. "How is it complicated? You have to act. You're a *star*, Morgan."

"Exactly!" I said. "And if you haven't noticed, I've got the paparazzi up my butt twenty-four-seven, watching my every move. What do you think they're going to say about me trying out for *Oklahoma!*?"

"Lame," Riley said, his mouth full of sandwich.

"See?" I said to Delia.

"No," Riley said. "*You're* lame. If you don't want to be in the play, don't be in the play. But using the press as an excuse? Come *on*. You're a better actress than that."

I asked him what he meant and he said, "I think you're *dying* to try out. I think nothing would make you happier than to show girls like Debbie Ackerman exactly what you're made of."

Now it was my jaw on the table.

"Don't look surprised, Morgan. Your rivalry with Ms. Ackerman is entirely public."

"I don't know if I like you," I said, shifting in my seat.

Riley grinned. "Sure you do. But my guess is you can't admit that either, in case word gets back to your boyfriend, Eli. He *is* still your boyfriend, right?"

"You're kind of weird," Delia said to Riley.

"You're kind of cute," he shot back.

The first thing I thought was, *I have never in my life seen*

Delia's face turn so red! The second thing? *Hey, what about me?*

"Don't worry," Riley said, as if reading my thoughts. "I think you're cute, too."

Riley and I traded barbs the rest of the lunch period, but I couldn't stop thinking about what he'd said. Was I really *dying* to show off my acting chops? I mean, yeah, I did want to get back at Debbie Ackerman, and I'm sure it would burn her toast if I were to land the lead in *her* school play. But Riley made it sound like I wanted to give everyone the finger, and not just Debs. Was I really that petty? And if so, how come I was so transparent to this guy who, before today, I didn't even *know*?

Anyway, Riley did confirm what Delia had been trying to hammer into my head from day one: the spring musical is *muy importante* at this school. Like, *everyone* gets involved. Even the jocks try out, and supposedly, competition is fierce.

Even more importantly? Riley knew this because last year he'd been Conrad Birdie in *Bye Bye Birdie*—a junior beating out several pissed-off seniors for a seriously juicy part. *And* he's definitely trying out for *Oklahoma!*

Guess I better start practicing *my* audition piece, like, *stat*.

11/15—*Much later*

Oh. My. God.

This night has been completely surreal.

First of all, I took the bus home from school, which I pretty much never do, since the twins are always giving me rides. It felt weird. Weirder still was the fact that when I got off said bus, I found a very disheveled Emily Whitmarsh sitting on my front stoop.

Emily is a lot of things, but disheveled isn't one of them. So I knew something was wrong even before I got close enough to see the tear tracks on her cheeks.

"Em, what happened?" I asked.

She reached into the pocket of her jacket and pulled out half a dozen white things that looked like digital thermometers. Then she thrust them toward me. Imagine my surprise when I realized what they really were.

Home pregnancy tests.

I immediately felt sick to my stomach. Emily wasn't saying anything, just waving the sticks at me like I was supposed to take them from her. Which I did, once I was certain I wasn't grabbing anything that had been . . . er . . . wet.

Then I felt even more confused because every single one of them had a solitary blue line or a minus sign, and one even had the word *no* spelled out plain as day.

"I don't understand," I said. "You're upset because they're all negative?"

"No!" she cried. "I'm upset because I know they're *wrong*."

Since it was like thirty degrees outside, I handed Emily back her sticks and ushered her into the house, where I immediately started brewing a pot of coffee. "I take it you can still have caffeine, seeing as you're not actually pregnant, right?" I joked.

Emily wasn't amused.

We sat at the dining room table. I asked Em why she thought she was pregnant, and she immediately started to cry.

"We did it," she sobbed. "Caspar and me."

"And?"

"And we *did it*," she repeated. "Saturday night. *Twice*."

She was crying so hard I had to get up and grab her a box

of tissues. While I was up, I remembered Em telling me once that she had to go on the Pill when she was twelve because of irregular periods. So I said, "I thought you were on the Pill."

"I am." She punctuated the sentence with an ear-popping nose blow.

"And I know you're not dumb enough to do it with some college boy without insisting he wear a condom."

"He did," she said. "I even bought the stupid thing."

"Okay," I said. "Then I'm really, really confused. Because Em—you have to know, even if it broke, the odds of you getting pregnant while still on the Pill are, like, slim to none."

"It didn't break," she sobbed.

My patience was beginning to thin. "Can you please explain to me then why you're so convinced that you're pregnant?"

Emily hiccuped a few times and pressed a third tissue to her bright red nose. "Because I *did it*," she said again. "*Twice.*"

"So I've heard." I sighed. "Let me guess—it was your first time?"

She nodded, and a million thoughts swirled through my brain.

Most of them about *my* first time. All of them completely unwanted.

"What did he do?" I asked, my eyes boring into hers. "Did he force you?"

"Who, Caspar?" Emily shook her head again. "No, he was a perfect gentleman. He even sent me flowers yesterday. Do you know how hard it is to find a florist who has Sunday hours?"

Here I had to remind myself that Emily has been a good friend to me and that even if I couldn't figure out what her issue was, I could *not* let myself give her a good shake.

So instead, I went into the kitchen and poured us both mugs of coffee with Splenda and extra creamer. When I got back, Emily had settled down some. Not much, but enough that her sentences were getting close to coherent.

"I feel like such an idiot," she said, sniffling.

"Yeah," I said, "if I'd wasted fifty bucks buying pregnancy tests, I'd feel pretty dumb too."

Em shot me the evil eye and then—finally—she started to chuckle. And eventually the chuckle turned into a laugh. And then we were both laughing for a bit. . . .

And then Em started crying again.

When I got her to calm down the second time, she said, "I'm not supposed to do things like this, you know. I'm a 'good girl.'"

I said, "What, and good girls don't ever want to get a little?"

"You don't understand," she said. "We haven't even been going out a full six *weeks*."

I asked her what would've been an appropriate time frame—what makes the difference between a sensible teenage girl having sex and a wanton underage slut engaging in sin.

When she didn't respond, I said, "Em—if you bought the condoms yourself, you must've been thinking about it, right? Taking precautions? Doing what *real* good girls do—being responsible."

"So what happens now?" she asked. "We keep doing it, right?"

I shrugged. "Unless you don't want to."

When Emily didn't respond, I said, "*Do* you want to?"

She sighed. "I don't know. Some of it was good. Other parts were just . . . messy. I felt like—clumsy and awkward. How long before it stops feeling like that?"

I shrugged again. "Until you get it right?"

I thought that would be the end of the conversation. But Emily frowned and said, "You're holding back, Morgan, and I don't appreciate it. I help you with your geometry, don't I? Now it's your turn to help me."

"Help you with what?" I asked.

"You know," she said. "*Sex.*"

She said this last word in kind of a whisper, and it took me a few beats to realize she wasn't joking.

"You seriously think I can tutor you in *sex*?" I yelped.

Em shook her head. "No, not like that. But you must know about these things, right?"

I sucked in a breath. I couldn't believe what she was saying.

"Why?" I said. "Why would I know about them? Is it because if you're a 'good girl,' then I must be a bad one?"

"No!" Emily cried. "That's not what I'm saying. It's just that—"

"You thought I was a slut," I finished for her. "Right?"

"Experienced," she said. "I thought you were experienced."

Oh, the irony.

"Well, I'm not," I said testily. "In fact, you're probably more 'experienced' than I am, okay?"

Emily's eyes widened, like she couldn't believe what I was saying. It made me even angrier—at first.

But then I realized that it wasn't such a huge jump to make. I mean, I didn't respect my body when it came to taking drugs or drinking—or even eating when I was supposed to. Why would I respect it enough not to sleep around?

Em tried to apologize, but I waved her off.

"Forget about it," I said. "It's just a sore subject is all."

Understatement of understatements.

Emily was still clutching the used pregnancy tests, so I went and got a trash can and made her throw them out. Then I said, "Instead of feeling sorry for yourself, maybe you should try being a little happy. I mean, your first time was with a sweet guy you really like and who practically worships the ground you walk on. Even if it wasn't perfect, a lot of girls—one in three, if I remember correctly—lose their virginity in some kind of date-rape situation."

I could feel my face growing hot, turning red. I turned away from her and took a deep breath before I continued.

"So, you know. You beat the odds, at the very least."

She was quiet for a minute. Then she said, "Is that what happened to you?"

I'd kind of known I'd tell her eventually.

About Harlan Darly and how he got me stoned and then forced himself on me when I was the ripe old age of fourteen. About how, even after I told Ms. Janet Moore about the incident, I thought I was the one to blame since I'd not only been drunk and high but also flirting with him.

I mean, he was *Harlan Darly*. He'd hooked up with supermodels, A-list actresses, one of the Bush twins—the blond one, I think. It was so exciting, the way he looked at me, and how he'd make up any excuse to touch me, like say I had a smudge of something on the corner of my mouth just so he could wipe it away. . . .

"Is that what happened to you, Morgan?" Em repeated.

I nodded slowly. And then, over the next half hour or so, I told her all about Harlan Darly.

Emily threw her arms around me, and her hug made most of the bad feelings melt away.

"I remember thinking it was weird, at Debbie's slumber party, how you kept saying Harlan Darly was an ass-hole," she said. "Now I understand. No wonder you hate the guy."

I felt drained. Really drained.

Then Em said, "Have you told Eli that story?"

"*No,*" I replied sharply. "And don't you even think about repeating it to him."

"I won't," she swore. "Not if you don't want me to. It's just that—"

"I don't want him to know," I cut her off. "There's no reason for him to know."

"Except that he thinks you're . . . I don't know. Worldly?"

"Slutty," I deadpanned. "The Hollywood Whore."

Em shook her head. "Experienced," she said again, ever the diplomat. "Maybe even . . . skilled. I mean, that picture of you with your top off—"

I told her I didn't want to talk about it anymore and reminded her of what she'd said earlier—about not wanting to be a part of Eli's and my relationship.

That did the trick. She agreed, finally, to stay out of it.

When Trudy got home, we decided to order Chinese. Emily ate with us. She still looked sort of freaked after din-ner, so I asked her if she wanted to stay over.

"But it's a school night," she said.

"I know," I said, "and we go to the same school, remem-ber? Just tell your mom you're tutoring me for a big test or something. She can't possibly think I'm capable of corrupting you within a few hours' time, especially with Trudy around."

Now Emily is snoring loudly on the couch and I'm completely wide awake. I'm an insomniac by nature, but the last time I relived the Harlan Darly experience, I didn't sleep for three days.

And when I did sleep, I had nightmares. Bad ones.

Although I have to admit it's getting easier to talk about it. Like the drugs, I suppose. I used to get so embarrassed, those first few days at Crapplewood. But then I realized everyone there had the same kinds of embarrassing problems, and learning how to talk about them—how to be comfortable talking about them, even—is like reclaiming something you lost.

Who would've thought that owning your mistakes could be so oddly empowering?

11/16

Instead of listening to Mr. Garrett's mind-numbing lecture about Dante's *The Divine Comedy*, I spent most of English class trying to figure out who I was going to sit with at lunch.

Yes, I really am that shallow.

I wanted to sit with Riley, but Emily was still looking fairly fragile from her non-pregnancy scare. How could I get her to come with me without making it look like I was asking her to choose sides?

Plus, how would she react to me flirting with a boy who wasn't her brother?

Am I flirting with a boy who isn't her brother? Hmmm.

As Garret kept blathering on about the "celebrated" epic

poem (translation: long-ass thing that was written a hundred million years ago), I decided to chuck Dante's *Inferno* and create my own version of hell. Here it is:

MORGAN CARTER'S NINE CIRCLES OF HELL

#1 QVC hostesses

#2 Shania Twain fans

#3 Celine Dion fans

#4 Dr. Phil

#5 My mother, after she's had about three gin and tonics

#6 My mother, before she's had *any* gin and tonics

#7 The entire cast of *7th Heaven* (except Happy—I kinda like the dog)

#8 The Federlines (some people should *not* be allowed to breed)

#9 Harlan Darly

So I guess maybe I absorbed something after all.

11/16—*Later*

I just want to note for the record that it has been *three* solid days without any kind of contact from Eli whatsoever. Even if he wasn't my boyfriend—even if all we were ever supposed to be is friends—shouldn't he have called by now? We got in a fight—a sort of ugly one—and it's like . . . like he doesn't even *care*.

Meanwhile, it takes a soul-sucking amount of effort every single day to pretend that I don't care about him not caring. Please! My best friend is his twin sister.

How many times have I wanted to demand that Emily

spill it? I don't think they've invented numbers that high. But she's so careful about not even saying his name around me that really, I have no idea what's going on.

Emily update: Caspar has left seven messages on her cell, all of which she's let go unreturned. When I asked her why, she said, "I'm not ready to talk about it." I thought she meant she wasn't ready to talk to *me* about why she didn't want to talk to *him*, but then she continued, "How does anybody ever talk about it without feeling like a total idiot?"

By "it," I realized she meant "sex."

I told her I'd never actually talked to a guy about "it" before. "Hell," I said, "these days I can't seem to talk to anyone about anything." I gave her a sideways glance, hoping she'd take pity on me and divulge a little something about the Eli situation, but she called me on it immediately.

"I can't," she said, without me even having to ask. "If it makes you feel better, I refuse to talk to him about you too."

"So he's asking about me?" I asked, but all she said was, "Nice try."

11/16—*Even later*

To: Marissa Dahl
From: Morgan Carter
Subject: Chicks and dudes and geeks better scurry. . . .

Dear M.,

Forget stretch limos and modified Hummers. Want to know the latest mode of transportation to which I aspire?

Surrey with a fringe on top, baby.

Yes, it's true. I've decided to audition for the school's

"spring" musical (ironic quotes added because I just found out the show traditionally goes up the same weekend as Martin Luther King Day, which, as you probably know, is in *January*). This year's masterpiece is going to be *Oklahoma!*, and I'm fixin' to play Laurey, the farmer's daughter whose heart is torn between a cowboy and a field hand. *Do not make any jokes*. According to my new friend Riley, the play's a big deal at Snider. And I think I already told you about how that beyotch Debbie Ackerman keeps spreading false rumors about me. (I can't wait to kick her ass all over that stage!)

Not all is well in Morgan land. I have some bad news on the boy front: it looks like me and E. might be over before we even began. I don't feel like going into it via e-mail, but if/when you get this message and you feeling like chatting, give me a ring. I'm still using the bling-bling cellie you bought me for my birthday, same number and everything. Give me a holla, yo.

Peace out,
the other M.

11/17

Just got off the phone with Bianca. I hadn't heard from her since she made the abbreviated call from that chichi salon last week. Hadn't heard from Sam either, though I'd left him at least a dozen messages over the past few days.

"I take it you've seen the pictures," Bianca said, disappointment dripping from every syllable.

Of course I'd seen them. Me and Eli making out from about seven different angles—plus the bra shot.

I'd only ever seen myself kissing someone on film, where the director makes things look all pretty. But when two people are kissing in real life, it's way less attractive. You can see Eli's tongue in a couple of shots, and my cheeks are pulled in tight like I'm suctioning his lips to my own.

"Please don't lecture me," I said. "I tried to call Sam to warn him, but he never called me back."

"I don't think you made it clear to him how important it was for him to return your calls," she said dryly. "I mean, for God's sake, Morgan! What the hell were you wearing? And why aren't you using that new skin cream I sent? I haven't seen you with so many zits since you were detoxing."

Okay, first of all? Those pictures were way too blurry for her to have been able to identify my blemishes. What was she doing, studying them under a microscope?

"Wait," I said. "You're mad because I don't look cute enough?"

Bianca sighed. "Your image is still important, Morgan. Just because you're in Fort Wayne doesn't mean we want you being photographed looking like a frump."

I couldn't have been more confused. I thought I'd get in trouble because the hacks caught me and Eli in a clinch. But I never, ever thought Bianca would be pissed at me because of how I *looked*.

"You're the one who told me keep wearing Old Navy!" I accused. "I was the one who wanted my wardrobe back!"

"It's not about what you wear," she said sharply. "It's about how you wear it. If Sharon Stone can make best-dressed lists wearing a Gap T-shirt to the Oscars, you can certainly find a way to wear Old Navy with panache.

"You're no longer Claudia Miller," she continued. "And we

think it's high time you start carrying yourself like the Morgan Carter you were raised to be."

"You mean *trained* to be, right?" I said, not caring if I sounded bitter. If I did, Bianca certainly didn't notice—or at the very least didn't care.

"I need you to clear your schedule for the rest of the week," she informed me. When I asked why, she said, "I'm hiring you a personal trainer. I'll let you know where you need to be and when."

I reminded her that I don't have a car—or a driver's license—for that matter. This, however, did not deter Mama Bianca.

"Not a problem," she said. "I'll arrange for car service as well. And until you've had about a month at the gym, I suggest you keep your clothes *on*."

I sighed. So much for life as a normal teenager.

"This photo spread was quite a surprise—and you know how much I like surprises," she added, her voice deep-fried in sarcasm. "Is there anything else you've neglected to fill me in on?"

I briefly considered telling her about what happened with Eli but decided against it. She'd have told me I needed to be focusing on more important things, like daily facials or whatever.

Instead, I told Bianca I was trying out for *Oklahoma!* next week. I thought it might make her chuckle, but she cried, "Morgan Carter! Why would you do *that*?"

"I . . . thought it would be . . . funny?" I answered slowly.

Bianca sounded alarmed. "What were you thinking? How is it going to look? A Hollywood actress stealing the

69

lead in a high school production—have you even bothered to check with Sam about this?"

I could feel my lips curling into a wicked grin. I hadn't heard her this riled up in a good, long time. "Breathe, Mother," I deadpanned. "Remember to breathe."

"Never mind," Bianca snapped. "I'll take care of this. But you are *not* trying out for this play."

"You can't stop me," I said, sounding like some stupid sitcom teen.

Bianca said, "You still don't get it, do you? You have some warped notion that you're living in obscurity. Well, missy, let me tell you: you're not. All eyes are on you right now, and you can't make a single false move. One misstep and you might as well kiss your career good-bye."

Pressure, anyone?

"And by the way, I'm FedEx-ing you a ticket home for Thanksgiving," she said.

This despite my well-articulated wishes to remain in Indiana for the four-day break.

"I specifically told you that I didn't want to go to California," I said. "I specifically and repeatedly asked that you and Sam come *here*."

"Yes, but that was before," she replied.

"Before what?"

"Before we got the invite from John and Kelly."

John and Kelly . . . as in *Travolta* and *Preston*.

"Oh God," I groaned. "They're so industry. I thought Thanksgiving was supposed to be about *family*. As in us. *Alone*."

"This *is* about family," Bianca said. "Your stepfather—"

"Sam," I cut in.

"*Sam*," she repeated, "who is now your *stepfather*, needs to expand his client base. And I have it on good authority that Neil Patrick Harris will be in attendance at the Travoltas'. According to Ca-RAY, he's seeking new representation. It's a perfect fit."

"Doogie Howser?" I practically screeched. "You're ruining my Thanksgiving break because your colorist has convinced you that Sam might possibly run into Doogie *freaking* Howser? Jesus, who's next? The Karate Kid?"

"Ralph? No. I hear he's very happy with his manager."

I sighed heavily. "Thank you for completely missing my point."

We went a few more rounds before Bianca said, "Four months ago, you were literally on your knees begging me not to export you to Fort Nowhere and now this? I'm offering you a first-class plane ticket home and entrance to the hottest Thanksgiving dinner in town. What more could any sixteen-year-old girl ask for?"

"Nothing," I said, because that's what she wanted to hear. "Except I turned seventeen last month, remember?

Now it was Bianca's turn to sigh. "I don't know why I bother, Morgan. I will never be good enough for you, will I?"

I wanted to say, "Right back at ya," but I knew exactly where that would lead: to another hour of bickering. In the end, she'd still get her way and I'd still be slated to spend Turkey Day at the Travoltas'.

"Before I go, one more thing," Bianca said. "You need to watch *Leno* tonight."

"Why? Who's on?"

"Just do it, Morgan. For Pete's sake! Why must you question *everything*?"

Then she hung up without even saying goodbye.

11/17—Later

So, guess who else finally bothered to call?

"We need to talk," Eli said.

I decided to play it cool. "About . . . ?"

"About us," he said.

ME: What about us?

ELI: Is there still an us?

ME: Gee, I don't know, Eli. You tell me. I mean, you're the one who wanted to slow things down to begin with.

ELI: Right. Slow, not stop. Besides, you're the one who stormed out of Casa's on Saturday.

ME: And you're the one who didn't come after me! Or call! Or say so much as "boo" for four solid days!

ELI: How could I say anything to you when every time I see you, you're with that guy?

ME: Who, Riley?

ELI: The senior you've been eating lunch with all week.

ME: I would've been more than happy to introduce you to him.

ELI: Morgan . . .

ME: *Eli.*

ELI (sighing): I miss you, Morgan.

ME:

ELI: Did you hear me?

ME: Yeah, I heard you.

ELI: And?

ME: And I miss you too.

Before things could take a turn for the mushy, my call waiting beeped. "Hold on a second," I told Eli. I clicked over and found *Riley Augustine* on the other line.

"Were your ears burning?" I asked him. "I was just talking about you."

"Be honest," he teased. "You're always talking about me."

I smiled into the phone, then paused. "Wait a second. . . . How did you get my number?"

"I'm a professional stalker," he quipped.

"Not funny," I said. "Seriously, how did you—?"

"Relax," he said. "I chatted up your friend Delia Lambert. She has a serious hetero crush on you."

"You think?" I said with a chuckle. But simultaneously, I let out a sigh of relief. I wouldn't put it past the tabs to publish Trudy's unlisted number. They had gotten their hands on Nicky Hilton's cell phone number just last week. I could only imagine the frat boys who were ringing her line right at this moment.

"So what's up?" I asked, recovering.

He said, "Nothing much. I was just thinking that maybe you and I could hang out sometime."

"Hang out?" I asked. "Or go out?"

"We couldn't *go* out," he said. "Not while you still have a boyfriend, anyway."

Right, I thought. *Eli.*

Oh God. Eli!

"Shit!" I said. "I have to go. There's someone on the other line. Can we talk about this over lunch tomorrow?"

"Sure thing," he said.

When I clicked over, Eli had already hung up. So I called him back.

"Who was that?" he asked. "Your mom?"

"No," I said. "It was just . . . a friend."

"*Oh*," Eli said. "Your new friend, right? The senior?"

This pissed me off, and I didn't hesitate in letting Eli know.

"Look," I said. "You're the one who didn't want anything to be 'official.' So even if I was interested in Riley—which I'm not—you have no right to be angry with me."

Eli was silent for a minute. If I hadn't heard him breathing softly, I'd have thought he hung up.

Finally, he said, "So let's go out. Officially."

I'd be lying if I said my heart didn't give a little leap. Still, I wasn't sure if I wanted what Eli was offering.

"Is this a jealousy thing?" I asked. "You see one guy talking to me and suddenly everything's changed?"

"No," he said. "I mean, okay, *yes*. I'm jealous that you're spending time with that Riley guy. But that's not why—"

"What about your mother?" I said, cutting to the chase. "What about everything you said at Casa's?"

"Things have been pretty crazy around our house lately, what with those photos and all."

"Right," I said, feeling my face flush. "I'm sorry about that."

"Don't be," he said. "This is not your fault. I knew what I was getting into. I mean, after I found out about you being . . . you know . . . *you* . . . I just didn't know how to handle it."

I needed to level with him. "It's not going to get any easier," I said.

"I know. And that's part of the problem," he went on. "Those jerks staking out the house, reporters calling on a

74

regular basis . . . I know it's worse for you. And that's what's got my mom so concerned. She's worried that under all this pressure, you're going to relapse or something."

That made the hairs on my neck stand up. "Well," I said tightly, "you can tell her that this concern of hers? It's unfounded, unwarranted, and unappreciated."

"Morgan," Eli said softly. "She doesn't mean it as an attack. Her concern for you is sincere. And her concern for me is that I'll end up falling for another girl who . . . has to leave."

I paused.

Right. The ex again.

Just over a month ago, Claudia Miller, my small-town alter ego, had been enough to make Eli forget all about his epic heartbreak.

But me? Morgan Carter? Apparently that's another story.

"I told you I'm not leaving," I said firmly. "Not for rehab. Not for anything. I don't care what Bianca says—or even Sam. I'm happy here. I'm—I'm here to stay. Don't you get that?"

"I do," Eli said, "most of the time."

"Listen," I said. "I'm really tired, and my mom told me I need to watch *Leno* tonight—don't ask me why, because she didn't say—and anyway, I was hoping I could take a nap before it comes on. So I've got to go."

"All right. But . . . are we okay?" Eli asked.

"I'm not sure," I said. "But we can talk more tomorrow. Over lunch?"

"I'd like that," he said. "Sweet dreams, you."

I felt a shiver run through me as I hung up the phone. Then I felt a need to write it all down.

So guess what? No nap for me.

And now it's time for *Leno*.

11/17—*Much later*

Oh. My. *God*.

There's no reason for me to have nightmares in my sleep. I actually get to *live* one.

When Bianca told me I needed to watch *Leno* but wouldn't tell me why, I got online to see who was scheduled to appear. It was supposed to be Caroline Rhea, pimping some reality show where they make fat people do stupid things like sit in a room full of cupcakes and not eat them, and Emmet Swimming, a D.C.-based band whose latest single has been on the radio nonstop.

Since Bianca's idea of good music consists solely of vintage Barbra Streisand and Neil Diamond records, I figured she wanted me to see Caroline Rhea. Probably her twisted way of reminding me to watch my figure.

So imagine my surprise (horror!) when, at the end of his monologue, Jay's list of guests included *Harlan Darly*.

Now, I never told Bianca what he did to me, so I was hoping that if he was the one she wanted me to see, it was simply because he was a former co-star. But of course, that was overly optimistic.

Because when Harlan Darly sat in Jay's guest chair, he spent about two minutes talking up his latest project, a date movie so lame even Ashton Kutcher would've passed on it (and probably did!).

Then he proceeded to spend the rest of his interview *talking about me*!

It started innocently enough, with Jay asking him if he had some special lady in his life. I snorted, hoping for the sake of womankind that he didn't.

Harlan flashed his famous "aw shucks" grin, lowered his gaze, and said, "No, no. No one at the moment."

Then Jay said, "Now, why is that? A good-looking guy like you, I'd think you'd be beating them off with a stick."

"Well, to be honest, Jay," Harlan replied, "I'm nursing a bit of a broken heart."

The studio audience let out a collective "awww," and you could literally see a bit of blush creep into Harlan's cheeks. I sat transfixed, wondering if it was possible that he'd turned into an actual human.

I always thought you had to *have* a heart for it to be broken.

"Who is she?" Jay asked. "Who is this creature who stole your mojo?"

If hearing Jay Leno say the word *mojo* wasn't disturbing enough, Harlan repeated the grin/head-dunk thing and said, "I shouldn't. . . . You guys don't really want to know about that, right?"

A mix of applause and whistles erupted from the audience; Harlan waved his hands around as if to say, "Oh, you guys. Go on."

"We won't rest until we get a name," Jay quipped.

Harlan reached forward and picked up his glass of water and gulped about half of it down. Then he said—I kid you not—

"This is kind of embarrassing, Jay. But it's—it's Morgan Carter."

My stomach lurched and, thinking I was going to puke, I hit pause on the TiVo and ran to the bathroom.

"Trudy!" I screamed once the nausea was under control. "Trudy, get out here!"

She rushed out from her bedroom, tying the belt of her robe.

"What is it?" she asked, alarmed. "What happened?"

I hit rewind until I reached the part where Jay first asked Harlan about his love life.

Trudy gasped and said, "Is that who I think it is?"

"Just watch," I said, my voice barely above a whisper.

By the time I heard Harlan say my name again, tears had filled my eyes and were starting to fall. Trudy grabbed the remote from me and hit pause again.

"What is this?" she demanded. "Is this some kind of sick joke?"

"I don't know," I said. "I stopped watching here."

I should've told her about Bianca's call earlier today, but things have been really strained between Trudy and Mama B. lately. Mostly because Trudy resents Bianca's attempts to rob me of what's left of my childhood, but also because Bianca's gotten totally jealous of how close Trudy and I are.

At any rate, I didn't want add more fuel to the fire.

"Are you okay?" Trudy asked me, wrapping my hands in hers.

I nodded. "Let's just watch the rest."

She hit play.

"Morgan Carter!" Jay exclaimed. "Now, how did *that* happen?"

Harlan told him about us doing that movie together a

few years back. Then he said, "I felt this . . . bond with her. You know? We had this amazing friendship and . . . well . . . I've never stopped thinking about her."

As the audience launched into another collective "awww," I momentarily lost the ability to breathe.

"No," Trudy said. "This can't be happening."

"Let me get this straight," Jay said. "You are talking about *the* Morgan Carter, right? Doesn't she have some midwestern boy toy?"

Harlan nodded gravely. "Hence the broken heart. I thought that maybe, one day, we'd be together. But she seems happy, Jay. And I want that for her, so—"

"I can't take any more," I said to Trudy. "Please, just . . . turn it off."

She complied with my request.

"Why?" she asked after a moment. "Why would he say that? I mean, didn't you tell me you haven't so much as seen him in two years?"

I shook my head. "I don't know," I said. "Maybe he's trying to get publicity for his new movie."

Trudy looked incredulous. "How does *this* help his movie?"

I gave a bitter laugh. "The tabloids are going to have a field day with it. They'll paint it like some kind of love triangle. They're probably hard at work right now, sitting in their tiny little offices, Photoshopping pictures of me and . . . and *him*. Making it look like we had a past." I paused. "It'll be the biggest story of the week."

"Oh, Morgan." Trudy folded me into her arms. She held me while I cried—until I snotted up the shoulder on her terry-cloth robe. She told me I didn't have to go to school

79

tomorrow if I didn't want to, but I told her that was out of the question.

"If I don't show up, they'll talk even more," I said. "Besides, there's Eli. Things will be even worse for him now. I guess I should warn him."

Trudy took my chin in her hands, tilted my head so I was looking directly into her eyes. "Morgan. It's not Eli I'm worried about."

"I have Emily," I told her. "She knows about . . . you know."

Trudy nodded. "I'm glad," she said. "She's a good friend."

She offered to make us both some tea, but I said no, I needed to get to bed.

That was almost five hours ago, and I haven't slept a wink.

11/18

In my post-*Leno* haze, I totally forgot what Bianca had said about me needing to clear my schedule. So it was kind of a surprise that when Trudy and I left the house this morning there was a Lincoln town car waiting for me out front. A driver, fully decked out in a black suit, skinny tie, and one of those driving caps with the patent leather visor, emerged. He didn't say a word, just opened the door to the backseat and waited patiently for me to get in.

I looked at Trudy, but she just shrugged. So I turned back to the driver and said, "Did my mother hire you?"

He shut the car door and approached, his right hand outstretched. That's when I noticed he was even wearing pearl gray gloves. Seriously! The guy looked so money that I felt like a mafia princess or something. Anyway, he introduced himself as Thaddeus Maplethorpe the Third, which made me giggle almost immediately.

I mean, come on! With a name like that, the guy should've been a trust fund baby, sailing to Bora-Bora with a boat full of champagne-and-caviar-fed supermodels just for kicks.

My giggling made Thaddeus's brow furrow ever so slightly, and I instantly felt rude. I didn't want to offend the guy, so I shook his hand in return and said, "Hey, I'm Morgan, and this is my guardian, Trudy." Thaddeus pulled an official-looking document from his inside breast pocket. A piece of cream-colored stationery with the initials BLR was stapled to the top. (Bianca Liana Rosenbaum. *She must've finally dropped the Carter from her name*, I thought.)

The letter was brief; its sole purpose—beyond verifying that yes, Bianca had ordered this particular driver—was to tell me that if I didn't comply with the attached schedule, my "emergency" MasterCard would be canceled and I wouldn't see a cash allowance until February of next year.

"Do you believe this?" I fumed to Trudy after reading her the contents of the note.

"Your mother has always had a . . . unique . . . parenting style," she said. Then she glanced at her watch. "Morgan, honey—I gotta go. I've got an early meeting. Why don't you give Sam a ring on the way to school? He'll straighten this out."

She gave me a quick kiss on the temple and hopped into her Saturn before I could remind her that California was three hours behind us time-wise and I wouldn't be able to get ahold of anyone until lunch.

Thaddeus reopened the back door, and I climbed in. The schedule Bianca had arranged for me was ridiculous. In addition to the personal trainer, she'd scheduled me to meet with a voice coach, a dance teacher, a yoga instructor, a nail technician, and a hair stylist.

Like today: after school, I was to report immediately to someone named Veronique for a two-hour singing lesson. From there, I had thirty minutes to hydrate and get across town to the Fort Wayne Dance Collective, where I'd receive another two hours of instruction. Then I had a forty-five-minute break, during which I was to eat a salad sans dressing *or* a veggie omelet made with egg whites that Thaddeus would pick up for me while I was at dance (she's so much of a control freak, she even told him *where* to procure this rabbitine dinner). The last stop of the evening was the Beyond Personal Training Studio, to meet with some dude named Fabrizio for ninety minutes of cardio and strength training.

After quickly adding up hours and minutes in my head, I realized I wouldn't even be finished up at the studio until 9:45 p.m. Assuming Thaddeus broke several speed limits, I should make it home around 10 p.m. I'd need at least a thirty-minute shower to recover, which would leave me maybe an hour and a half tops to complete my homework. But no. Bianca's schedule didn't account for homework.

I wanted to kill her. Especially after the Harlan Darly thing.

While I was lying in bed the night before, trying desperately to fall asleep, I realized that Bianca must've been involved. How else would she have known what he was

82

going to say? I wouldn't be surprised if she'd actually paid him to say it—her knowing as well as I did that this would keep my name and face in the tabs for several weeks to come.

Image, she'd said, *is still important.*

All of this was designed to improve my image. It totally fit together. All except the part about the voice teacher and the dance coach, that is.

As Thaddeus pulled up at Snider, I realized that I couldn't do half the stuff on that sheet anyway because it was Thursday, and I always—*always*—go to my NA meetings Thursday nights.

Tomorrow . . . well, I suppose I could indulge her and run through the paces, but no way am I giving up my entire weekend to this nonsense.

Anyway, you should've seen the look on Emily's face when she first walked into English this morning.

"Is it true?" she asked. "About *The Tonight Show?*"

I nodded. "This is Bianca's work. I'm sick about it."

"I can imagine," she said.

I asked her if Eli had heard about it too, and she didn't answer.

"Come on, Emily," I begged. "I need to know what he knows."

She told me she wasn't sure. "All I can tell you is that last night, he seemed a little happier."

I sighed, relieved.

"We talked," I told her. "Did he tell you?"

She said no, so I filled her in on our conversation. Em seemed happy enough—but like before was trying to remain neutral.

You have to respect that about her. The girl is like Switzerland.

Then the bell rang, and Mr. Garrett started his lesson.

Twenty more minutes of Dante and his insufferable *Inferno* before I can call Sam and make him tell me exactly what's going on.

11/18—*Later*

The minute I got out of English, I was on the cell, dialing Sam's office. His new receptionist, who sounds like a four-pack-a-day smoker, informed me that he was in a meeting and asked if she could take a message. I told her that I was Mr. Rosenbaum's stepdaughter and that if he didn't come to the phone immediately, I would be spending my eighteenth birthday posing for *Playboy*. Or *Penthouse*. Or both.

Smoky rushed off to inform her new boss of my intentions. It *still* took about five minutes of annoying hold music before I heard Sam's gravelly voice on the other end.

"Did it ever occur to you," he began, "that maybe *you're* the reason I can't hold on to a receptionist for longer than a couple of months?"

"Please," I shot back. "That one was tame and you know it."

Sam chuckled. "What do you need, Morgan? Money? I'll wire you a G if you promise not to say what I think you called to say."

"You need to put your wife on a leash," I snapped. "Seriously, Sam—I'm not kidding. Not only am I ditching the driver and feeding my 'schedule' to the shredder, I'm tearing up the plane ticket home. You don't want me in the same room with her, especially not after that BS with Harlan Darly."

"Slow down, kiddo," Sam said. "Darly was my idea."

I gasped, the wind knocked out of me.

Sam did this?

"What? *Why*?"

"I'm trying to sign him as a client, but his publicist wanted proof that being repped by me would be more than a lateral move. Translation: she wanted me to help her re-energize his image by linking him to you."

I closed my eyes. This wasn't, *wasn't* happening. Sam was the only person in my life who I could always count on—for anything. (Well, except for Trudy, that is.) While Mama Bianca was off spending my hard-earned cash on Botox and brow lifts, Sam was the one who covered my tracks, who knew my secrets, who bailed me out.

Now *he* was selling me out?

He sighed heavily. "I know I should've told you, kiddo, but Bianca—she was afraid of how you'd react."

"She was right," I said. "Jesus, Sam. I expect this crap from her. But you? How could you pimp me out to *Harlan Darly* without even asking how I felt about it?"

His answer surprised me.

"Business," he said. "I've got to be honest with you, kid: it hasn't been so good. This is a young man's game, and by industry standards, I'm a goddamned dinosaur. The plan was to sign some fresher talent. Kids whose careers are on the rise—like yours. Then this opportunity came along and—"

I snorted. "My career is pretty much in the toilet right now, but thanks anyway."

Then it hit me.

"Sam," I said, "am *I* the reason business isn't good? Did people think you couldn't handle *my* career?"

Silence.

Oh my God.

Finally, he said, "It's not you, Morgan. It's everything. Christ, I got married! Of course I'm going to be distracted."

But I knew the truth. I knew it without him having to say it. He'd lost clients after news of my overdose broke, and instead of recruiting new ones, he'd spent the next six months worried about my recovery.

This was my fault. And as disgusted as I was to have my name linked to Harlan's, somehow, I was going to have deal. I owed it to Sam.

Really, I owe him everything.

"Fine," I said, resigned. "But what's up with Mr. town car and this crazy schedule Bianca sent?"

"It's prep," he said. "For your audition."

Long story short? Bianca had a change of heart about *Oklahoma!* She and Sam agreed that live theater could be "just the boost my image needs."

"*Oklahoma!*, Morgan," Sam boomed, selling it hard. "It's so wholesome. So all-American! And who knows? Maybe we could spin it into a part on Broadway, like that Christina Applegate thing."

I wanted to refuse—out of principle. But then I reminded myself, I was practically getting permission to put Debbie Ackerman in her place.

Something I would truly relish doing—and doing well.

"Okay," I agreed. "I'll do it. But is there any way to tone down this thing with Harlan Darly? Because it's going to be a nightmare for Eli. They'll hound the hell out of him, and he's not going to know how to deal with it."

"He'll learn," Sam said. "You can teach him. After all, we've been through worse."

Ain't that the truth.

"Listen, kiddo, I've got to run. Good luck with the lessons. I'll give you a call over the weekend."

And that, as they say, was that.

Lunch was another kind of weird entirely.

Eli met me outside the caf and threw his arms around me like I was Ingrid Bergman about to leave Casablanca for good.

"Whoa," I said. "What did I do to deserve that?"

"Nothing in particular," he said, tugging me even closer. "Can't a guy express his affection publicly?"

I didn't think much of it, even though Eli's never been huge on PDA, until *Riley Augustine* joined us at our usual lunch table. I'd forgotten that I promised him we could talk today and was startled when he sat down without invitation.

"Hey, guys," he said, diving into his bagged lunch with gusto.

Eli averted his eyes.

"Riley," I said. "Look, Delia, it's Riley Augustine."

Delia just sat there, mouth agape, looking from Eli to Riley and back again.

Leave it to Em to save the day. She broke the silence, introduced herself to Riley, then introduced E. as well.

"Hey," Eli said, in that terse way guys have of saying hello to one another.

Then, with the atmosphere already awkward (not to mention tense!), Eli got a case of roaming hands.

They were on my knee, my shoulder, around my waist. . . .

At one point, I turned to him and said, "Someone's being a bit grabby today, huh?" I said it quietly and with a little smile, like, "Ho, ho! Isn't this cute?" but Eli's face fell and he put his hands back in his lap.

"Sorry," he said.

"No, no," I told him. "It's just . . . um . . . I'm just not used to you being so . . . touchy-feely?"

He spent the rest of the period frowning into his pizza bagel.

Meanwhile, Riley chattered on, grinning straight at me even as he flirted with Delia.

This prompted Emily to give me semi-worried looks, but I just shrugged, not knowing what to make of the situation or how to fix it.

When the bell rang, Eli asked me if we could hang out after school, and I filled him in on Bianca's schedule.

It also gave me a chance to ask about *The Tonight Show*.

"I heard stuff," he said. "But I figured it had something to do with your mom."

"Good!" I said. "Yes! That's exactly what it is. So don't you worry about anything. Or anybody."

"Yeah." He frowned again. "Is Riley going to start sitting with us every day now?"

"We're just friends," I told him. "You have to trust me. Okay?"

"Okay."

I gave him a quick kiss and dashed off to my next class.

Everything hurts. *Everything*. Holding this pen is excruciating. And my throat! I'll be sucking Thayers Slippery Elm lozenges from now until Easter.

Today has been all over the map—literally and figuratively. This schedule Bianca's got me on is beyond nuts. Especially since I made Thaddeus push the meeting with the trainer back so I could fit in my NA meeting. I needed it more than ever.

By the time I got home, Trudy was already asleep, though she did leave me a note apologizing for rushing off this morning and telling me that if I needed anything, I should wake her up.

I thought about it—I could've used the talk—but she looked so peaceful in her sleep that I decided it could wait until morning.

Then I started dialing Bianca, but I don't know why I bothered since I knew she wouldn't answer. I even tried to block the "send number" feature on my cell, but she's got some program on *her* cell that blocks all anonymous numbers. After the fourth voice mail message, I gave up and took a long, hot bath.

I can't tell you how happy I am that tomorrow is Friday. School is awful right now. Everybody's gossiping about the Harlan Darly thing. It's so incredibly painful to hear, too. I want to blurt, "We never had a bond! He *raped* me!" But even if I could be that brave and admit what the bastard did, I can't be sure that anyone would believe me.

Sometimes I'm not sure *I* believe me.

I know what Ms. Janet Moore said when I told her about what happened—how just because I was drunk and high didn't mean that Harlan had the right to do what he did. But to this day, I can't remember if I ever said no or if before, I had maybe encouraged him at all.

I mean, I had such the crush on him.

But then I think about how awful I felt after. Not like hangover awful, but psychologically awful.

And if I felt that awful, then I must not have wanted it to happen.

So how *did* it happen?

I don't think I'll ever know for sure.

11/19

I overslept my alarm this morning. But hey—at least I *slept*. Thankfully, I had trusty Thaddeus on hand to make sure I was up and at 'em just in time to get to school before first bell.

So now I'm wearing black yoga pants, my white sports bra, and a red hoodie. My hair is pulled into a messy scrunchie bun and—oh, *no*—I just realized I put on my pink and white Sauconys, and they so fully clash with the cherry-colored hoodie.

In other words, I look like total shit.

Of course, this is the day that some asshole photographer manages to infiltrate my school!

He was waiting for me in front of my locker, camera pointed at me like a weapon. At first I was confused because so far, Barke's kept really tight security around here. But then, after the flash had gone off I don't know how many times, I realized what was happening. Instinctively, I threw my hands up to shield my face and hollered, "Can somebody help me here?" But no one did anything except stand there and gawk. It wasn't until a string of obscenities streamed out of my mouth that I could get a teacher's attention. It was Ms. Kwan, my history teacher, who finally came to my rescue. She told the hack that the police were on their way and that if he wanted to avoid being arrested, he'd best vacate the premises immediately.

The dude snapped one final shot before sprinting off toward the south exit.

I thanked Ms. Kwan for her assistance, but instead of giving me one of her trademark smiles, she frowned and said, "I don't like what I saw here today."

"I don't either!" I exclaimed. "I didn't invite that guy in. You have to believe me."

She nodded, but her frown stayed firmly in place. Then she told me to hurry up and get to homeroom.

But first, I had to get into my locker. When I did, a dozen brightly colored Gerbera daisies spilled out at me.

Like magic, Eli appeared.

"Good morning," he said. "How are you holding up?"

I smiled at him. Pre-*Oprah*, I would have been thrilled over a gift from Eli. But things between us were still . . . strange.

I wanted him back in my life, but this roller coaster we were riding was making me uneasy. I never really knew what was coming around the bend. Or what would send Eli running for the hills.

"Hey," I said, gathering up the flowers. "This is a nice surprise. How did you—"

"Get in your locker?" he finished. "I've got my ways."

I filled him in on what had gone down with the photographer and Ms. Kwan's unexpected reaction.

"I'm starting to hate this place," I said. "People are so damned mean."

Eli pulled me into a hug, and for a minute, I was comforted. Then he said, "Things aren't so hot for me either. Apparently I'm supposed to have a drag race with Harlan Darly. Winner gets the pink slip to your heart." He grinned.

"That's not funny," I said. "I hate Harlan Darly. I hate that I'm linked to him like this. But most of all, I really, really hate that my mother somehow managed to drag *you* into it."

Then my cell phone started ringing, and as I fumbled through my bag for it, Eli said, "Sorry about that Harlan Darly crack. Trying to make light of things, you know?"

He planted a kiss on my cheek, told me he'd see me at lunch, and headed off to homeroom.

Like I said—*strange*.

When I finally answered my phone, I was hoping it was Bianca calling me back, but instead it was a reporter from the *L.A. Times*.

"Morgan Carter, Lin Chang calling. We're running a short feature about your relationship with Harlan Darly, and I was hoping I could get a quote from you."

"How did you get this number?" I demanded.

"A quote," she repeated, like she hadn't heard my question.

"Go screw yourself," I said. "There's a quote for you."

Of course Principal Barke showed up at that exact moment, and before I could ream Lin Chang out any further, he plucked the phone from my hand, snapped it shut, and said, "No cell phones during school hours, Miss Carter. You can pick this up from my office after last bell. And don't think I don't know about your little photo session this morning." He stormed off before I could even defend myself.

A dark cloud settled over my thoughts. First the hack in school, now the *L.A. Times*?

I couldn't help but wonder—how much bigger was this Darly thing going to get?

The kicker? Right after Barke stomped away, I heard giggling behind me. I turned just in time to see my good friend Debbie Ackerman having a grand old chuckle at my expense.

"What are you laughing at?" I said, turning my eyes into laser beams. I imagined them slicing through her until she was nothing more than a little pile of Debbie shreds.

Very *Scrubs* of me, no?

Debbie said, "Love the new look, Morgan. Can't wait to see it splashed across the tabloids rack at Kroger."

This from the girl who thinks it's cool to wear miniskirts even though her legs are so stubby she could hang out with Willy Wonka. Troll!

"Well, *Debbie*," I said, "I guess we can't all be fashionistas like you. Who knows? Maybe you could single-handedly bring sparkly butterfly clips back into style."

I expected some sort of reaction, but all I got from Debbie was a patient, amused smile.

"Sticks and stones, Morgan," she said, with a confidence that was starting to rattle me a bit. Then she leaned in close and said, "Let's see who's laughing when Eli gets sick of playing your lapdog and comes running back to me."

My eyes narrowed into slits despite myself. "He can't run *back* to you if he never was with you to begin with. And Deb? He wouldn't go out with you even if *I* begged him to. You're better off setting your sights on someone you might actually have a shot with, like . . . I don't know. Who's that guy on yearbook who looks like Screech from *Saved by the Bell*?"

But I still wasn't getting a rise from Debbie, and it was beginning to piss me off. Even more annoying was her smug attitude, oozing out from every oversized pore.

"You'll see," she said, in a singsong voice. "You will see."

See what? is what I want to know. What cards does she think she's hiding up her sleeve? And hasn't she seen the way Eli's been acting around me lately? Weird or not weird, the boy can't keep his eyes—or hands, for that matter—off me.

God, why does that girl get under my skin so badly? She's nobody. Her only aspiration in life, besides trying to steal Eli out from under me, is to go to a state school, get a job at a shitty local paper, and try to find some dude dumb enough to marry her.

I'd be surprised if she ever makes it out of the state, let alone the country.

I seriously don't want to be here today. I wonder if Thaddeus would rat me out if I asked him to take me home right this second. Actually, that's not a bad idea. I think I'll head Eli off at the caf and see if he wants to cut the rest of the day with me—maybe curl up on the couch with a couple of mindless DVDs.

Let's see what Debbie Ackerman makes of *that*.

11/19—*Later*

It didn't take much to convince Eli to ditch, and if Thaddeus disapproved, his blank face didn't show it. So Eli and I hopped into the Camry and headed toward Blockbuster, where I quickly scooped up the following:

- *Bring It On* (in honor of Delia—well, her and the adorableness of Kirsten Dunst);
- *Mean Girls* (to generate possible revenge schemes to hatch on Debbie Ackerman);
- *Can't Hardly Wait* (the ultimate teen movie of my generation).

Afterward, Eli said he had to stop off at the pharmacy for some toothpaste. I thought it was odd of him to make a toothpaste run in the middle of the day, because I assumed Mrs. Whitmarsh kept her family stocked in the stuff at home, and Eli could always use the tube at my house if he was having some kind of urgent dental hygiene issue. But he said he needed some kind of special organic toothpaste, so I was like, "Whatever."

Only it wasn't "whatever," because Eli didn't really go for toothpaste. I mean, he did buy some Tom's of Maine (strawberry-flavored—the kind they make for kids!), but that wasn't the *only* purchase Eli made.

I found this out about halfway through *Bring It On*. Eli wasn't even watching the movie, just rubbing my hand and nuzzling at my neck. I wasn't really in the mood—I mean, I like kissing Eli and all, but as I've mentioned, he's been . . . a little strange.

Still, after thirty minutes of relentless rubbing, nuzzling, and soft cheek/chin kisses, I gave in.

So there we were, kissing at a normal clip, when Eli suddenly got all intense about it. He leaned into me so that my back was pressed up against the throw pillows. I couldn't keep track of where his hands were. Then, about ten minutes into this, Eli rolled off the couch and pulled a blue-foil-wrapped *condom* out of his pocket.

"What is that?" I asked, even though I already knew the answer.

Eli wouldn't say the word. Instead, he kept thrusting the packet in my direction, like, "Here, you take it!"

"Eli, what the hell?" I said, knocking it out of his hands. "We're back together for, like, thirty seconds—and you think you can just jump my bones?"

"Well, no," Eli said. "I just . . . thought you wanted to."

"Why would you think that?" I asked.

"Because . . ." He shrugged. "I don't know. I just *did*."

I took a deep breath. "There are stages to these things, Eli. Or, at least, there should be. I am not ready for you and me to be . . . you know. *Doing it*. Especially not now, when everything still feels really fragile."

Eli didn't say anything, so I continued. "Plus, with all this bullshit about me and Harlan Darly, sex is the *last* thing on my mind."

Eli was quiet for a bit, but eventually he said, "Wow. I'm really sorry, Morgan. I just . . . I thought you would expect me to . . . you know. Try. I mean, *I've* never . . . not even close. But *you* . . ."

"But I *what*?" I said, my voice sharper than I intended. "What, Eli? What is it that you think I've done?"

When he didn't respond, I said, "Yeah, okay, you got me. I screwed the entire cast of *The Mighty Ducks*. Parts one through three. Twice."

"Okay, okay!" Eli said, holding up his hands in a sign of truce. "I'm sorry. Really. I just thought—"

"Thought I was a slut," I finished

"No," he said firmly. "Experienced. I thought you were *experienced*."

That sounded awfully familiar. God! What was with these Whitmarshes?

"Has Emily been coaching you or something? Because I think that's the exact word she used. And anyway, you're both wrong. Dead wrong." I hugged my knees to my chest. "Your sister probably has more 'experience' than I do, so why don't you take your stupid condom and give it to her?"

I watched the blood drain from Eli's face; I'd gone too far. It's one thing to yell at a guy for a premature condom purchase; it's another to tell him flat out that his sister's doing the deed.

"I should—I should go," Eli stammered.

"No, don't," I said. "Wait."

I caught his hand and pulled him back onto to the couch. "You wouldn't know this about me, but sex is . . . it's kind of a hard thing for me to talk about. I don't really want to get into it with you because . . . well, frankly, it's not your business. Not right now. But suffice it to say that I am not the girl that you and half the population of Snider High think I am. I'm actually quite . . . *chaste*."

Eli let out a big sigh, and I couldn't tell if it was one of relief or what, so I said, "I'm sorry if that disappoints you, but it's how I feel."

"No!" he said. "No, it's how I feel too. I think . . . slow is good."

"Yeah?" I said.

"Yeah," he said.

I took the condom from him and placed under the couch cushion, figuring Trudy would find it—like a little present to her and Dave. Then Eli and I curled up together and watched the rest of *Bring It On* without him trying to steal any more kisses or even cop a feel.

So I guess it was good that we had "the talk." Right?

Still, I can't stop thinking about how he was in the cafeteria yesterday—you know, with his hands all over me and stuff. And now this? It feels possessive, like E.'s trying to send a message to anyone and everyone: *I own her. She is mine.*

I don't like how that feels.

My hope is that with Eli it's largely subconscious and that once he begins to feel more secure, this newfound jealousy and possessiveness and premature condom purchasing will cease once and for all.

11/19—*Later*

Day two of Bianca's Boot Camp was almost worse than day one. Veronique had me doing sirens for ten minutes straight, and let me tell you—working my vocal range that way does not yield the most pleasant of sounds. Then she had me doing this awful breathing exercise where I was supposed to puff up my diaphragm with air and hiss it out as slowly as possible, sucking the diaphragm back in as I did so. It would've been fine if Fabrizio hadn't worked my abs so hard last night.

"You," he said, in his thick, sexy Italian accent, "have too soft right here, eh? No muscle, just . . . eh . . . you know, *soft*."

"You mean fat," I corrected him. "Blubber!""

He grinned. "You find funny in yourself. I like."

I wish I could say the same about Fabrizio. I mean, he seems like an okay guy, but he's about six-foot four and has a neck like a tree trunk, the skin of which is rippling with

98

bulging veins. In fact, he looks a little like the Incredible Hulk, minus the green. And then there's the unibrow. I mean, you'd think a man vain enough to get his chest and back waxed would know better. Then again, Fort Wayne isn't exactly a hotbed of metrosexuals.

When we moved over to the leg press, Fabrizio adjusted the position of my feet in the spongy roller thing. He tapped my ankle and said, "You no drink enough water. Too much Diet Coke, eh?"

"Coffee," I confessed. Big mistake. He spent the next thirty minutes lecturing me on how caffeine messes with your metabolism and insulin production or absorption or something. I kind of tuned him out after a while, since there's no way I'm giving up my grande Sumatras. Christ, it's not like I have any other vices left! Except chocolate. Which, Fabrizio informed me, is also evil.

"I thought they declared dark chocolate good for you," I said. "In moderation."

He shook his head. "These same doctors say wine good for your heart too. You no drink any alcohol. Not while you train."

I didn't bother to tell him I'm a recovering alcoholic/addict, but I was surprised to hear that a native Italian was so against the vino. "I thought they started you on that stuff when you were in diapers," I mused.

"Wine is for to cook," he said as he instructed me to stretch my right arm over my head while simultaneously reaching across my stomach with the left. "Not to drink. Drinking starves the muscles."

At the end of the workout, Fabrizio handed me a shaker full of foamy butter-colored stuff. Some sort of banana

99

protein shake, as he was now convinced that my muscles were severely starved. It tasted a little like chalk, but mostly like faux 'nana.

On the ride home tonight, I asked Thaddeus to turn the radio on since he's not much of a talker and I'm not much for silence, as that tends to be the perfect breeding ground for obsessive thoughts. As Thaddeus was trying to find a station that didn't play country or Christian rock, I realized that my bag was beeping. I dug through it until I found my pink crystal-encrusted cell phone, which I'd remembered to rescue from Barke's office before I left Snider (but not without a stern lecture from Barke about how he doesn't care that I'm some movie star; school rules still apply to me).

Anyway, there were two missed calls: one from Mama Bianca, one from Marissa.

Marissa!

Bianca's message was short but typical—"Tomorrow, at nine a.m., you'll meet with Tosha at The Surface. Thaddeus has the address. You're booked for a cut, color, and wax. They don't do facials there, but if you need one, call and let me know. Kisses, sweetheart!" Of course she failed to address anything I'd raised in my previous voice mails to her, but whatever.

Marissa's message was even shorter and more typical. All she said was, "Hey, slut! I'm in London now, getting ready to fly to San Fran. Call you when I'm stateside, 'kay? Oh, and I fully made out with Ewan McGregor. On camera, of course, but *yum*."

Which means that she somehow hasn't gotten wind of the Harlan Darly story. Otherwise, she would've made some inappropriately dirty joke about the two of us.

I was grateful that Lin Chang hadn't bothered to call back and that no other reporters had managed to snag the number to the cell.

Until, that is, I got home.

The second I walked through the door, Trudy said, "There's ice cream in the freezer." So I knew something bad had happened.

Turns out that there were about forty messages on our home answering machine. Mostly from reporters—everyone from the guy who covers Page Six of the *Post* to *The National Enquirer*.

"Don't worry," Trudy assured me. "We're getting a new number tomorrow."

Yeah. That's consolation.

"There's more," she said. "Do you want me to tell you about it?"

"Hit me," I said, heading into the kitchen for a pint of sugary medicine.

Turns out there was a whole story on the me-Eli-Harlan-Darly "love triangle" (I so called that one, didn't I?) on *Entertainment Tonight*. And in the new *Entertainment Weekly*, there was a Q&A with Harlan in which he repeated the sob story he spewed on *Leno*, about how I broke his heart and pretty much ruined any chance of him having a love life.

If only that were true.

Trudy and I polished off the pint of pistachio ice cream while watching part of a *What Not to Wear* marathon on TLC.

Usually when we do this, we editorialize everything Stacy and Clinton say. But tonight, we were relatively somber. We only made it through one-and-a-half episodes before calling it a night.

I guess I didn't realize how ridiculously anxious I've been.

But tonight I got the picture—loud and clear.

Just a second ago, when I was brushing my teeth, I threw up without any warning, spilling pistachio-green vomit into the pink sink. My throat burned and my eyes stung, and after rinsing my mouth, I sat down on the cold bathroom tile and let myself have a good, long cry.

God. I cannot wait for all this crap with Harlan Darly to be over.

Then everyone can just go back to paying attention to something other than me.

11/20

Trudy had to drag me out of bed this morning. She'd tried to stall Thaddeus by offering him coffee and doughnuts, but he told her that we were on a tight schedule and that he'd wait for me in the car.

First stop of the day: the salon. Tosha, the new hairdresser Bianca handpicked for me, turns out to be a late-twenty-something chick who I can only describe as colorful. She's got a long, oval-shaped face and spiky hair in shades varying from caramel to cornsilk. She's got really big, really pretty eyes, the lids of which sparkle with dark purple glitter shadow. And her lips—naturally full and not collagenated the way so many California girls' are—are slicked with bright fuchsia gloss. She's reapplied it twice since I got here, which was only an hour ago.

My arrival was somewhat humiliating. Seems Bianca called ahead and told them I was not to be given any complimentary beverage or Danish. And, in fact, she'd paid extra to have Tosha pick up a major bottle of Evian just for me. Tosha, for her part, seemed almost apologetic when she handed it to me. Then she told me quietly that she had some PowerBars in her purse if I got hungry at all.

(NOTE TO SELF: When shopping for Bianca's Chrismukkah presents, be sure to adopt her patented passive-aggressive attitude and select innocuous-looking items that are really intended to make her feel A) old, B) fat, and/or C) wickedly out of fashion.)

As Tosha was foiling in some lowlights, my cell phone started singing "Dancing Queen," which is the tone I've assigned Emily's cell. The apple-green-haired girl working the station next to Tosha's was kind enough to fish the phone out of my bag, but trying to put the earpiece close enough to my head without managing to rub dye on the crystal-encrusted case proved more than difficult.

Emily sounded hysterical from the get-go. Apparently Caspar showed up on her doorstep early last night and refused to leave until Emily would come out and talk to him.

Which led to Mother Whitmarsh asking a zillion questions as to why Emily instructed her not to let Caspar in. What happened? Were they broken up? Why hadn't she said anything?

Then, sometime in the second hour, Caspar went around back and pounded on the glass-paned door, shouting for all the neighborhood to hear that he didn't care if she never wanted *to sleep with him* again, but would she at least come out so he could talk to her?

"Get out!" I practically yelped. "He really said that?"

"Worse," Emily said. "*She* heard it."

I asked her if she was grounded until she was ninety. Em said, "Not exactly . . . but you and I need to talk. Like, as soon as possible."

Bianca's Boot Camp didn't allow for side trips to comfort freaked-out friends, but I figured that it wouldn't be too hard to get my mother to relax the rules a bit. I told Em I'd call her right back, then dialed Bianca's cell. When she answered—I guess she was back to accepting my calls now—she was on the elliptical, slightly out of breath. It was nothing compared to the gasp she let out when I said that Emily was having a dermatological emergency and needed some CO_2 resurfacing on her chin stat and asked if I could pretty please go with her for moral support.

"Absolutely," Bianca affirmed. "I'll get the new girl to make some calls and switch your appointments around, then fax the new schedule to Thaddeus's BlackBerry. You are a good friend, darling. I'm very proud of you."

When I'd showed Bianca my six-month sobriety chip, the only thing she said was that it was a shame it only came in yellow. But imagining me nursing Em through some painful dermabrasion? *That* makes her proud.

So I'd called Em back and told her to put on the Lycra and lace up her dancing shoes because as soon as my session with Tosha was over, she and I were taking the limo to the arcade for some serious Dance Dance Revolution.

"Not today," she said. Then she told me to call her cell when I was ten minutes away from the dog park at the far end of her neighborhood. She would meet me there.

"Why am I picking you up at the dog park?" I asked, but

either she didn't hear me or she pretended not to, because the next thing I knew, she'd already hung up.

Tosha was blow-drying my now high- and lowlighted, freshly trimmed hair when Thaddeus came up to me to announce my schedule changes. And announce he did. Because of the blow-dryer, I couldn't really hear him, so I kept saying, "What?" until he was practically screaming.

"Bianca moved your voice lesson to five! Dance is at seven! And you won't go see your trainer until tomorrow!"

Tosha turned the dryer off just in time for me to hear some trailing laughter that sounded mightily familiar. I felt sick as I turned around to see who it was.

Debbie Ackerman.

I tried to play it off. "What's so funny?" I asked.

She gave me this look of cool superiority mixed with amusement. "You're taking *voice lessons*?" she said. "To prepare for a *high school* play audition? Gee, Morgan, I know it's been a while, but didn't you, like, get nominated for an Oscar once upon a time?"

I sighed heavily. "What's your point?"

"It just seems sort of . . . I don't know. *Pathetic?* All of this prep . . . and for what? The Snider High spring musical?"

Of course it would look that way to her. But which was worse? Having her think that I was preparing for the audition or that my mother thought I was so out of shape and style she was forcing me to do all of this?

I tried to play it cool. "If you're so confident you're going to land the lead," I said smoothly, "then why do you care what kind of prep I do for my audition? I mean, if I'm as little of a threat as you've been saying . . ."

That made her mad. I could tell by the way her plump cheeks turned a dark bluish red.

"At least I don't have to *pay people* to help me get where I want to go," she huffed.

I ripped off the black protective smock I'd been wearing for hours, handed it to Tosha, and said, "We done here?"

She nodded and I said to Thaddeus, loud enough for Debbie to hear, "Bring the limo around. And give her a fifty-dollar tip, will you? Cash, please. The rest should go on the business account." Then I thanked Tosha and sauntered outside. It took all the self-restraint I had not to turn around to see Debbie's reaction, but Thaddeus saw it and assured me I'd achieved the look I was hoping for.

This has gone on long enough. I don't care how busy my schedule is: tonight I'm forging plans to finally give Debbie Ackerman what she deserves.

Screw her, anyway! I am, after all, an *actress*. So what if I'm taking some classes? I would've taken them eventually anyway. I mean, I can't *really* stay in Fort Nowhere forever. Can I?

Anyway, I'm writing this in the back of the limo, sitting outside the dog park, waiting for Emily to show. If she doesn't get here soon, I'm going to have to skip my vocal lesson, and then Bianca will really blow a gasket.

11/20—*Later*

I don't even know where to begin. Maybe with Emily hopping into the back of the limo, uncharacteristically wearing all black and a pair of dark-tinted sunglasses, even though it's another gray, twenty-degree day in Fort Lame.

"Tell him to go!" she whispered urgently, like she was Sydney Bristow or something.

I asked her where, and she said it didn't matter.

Then she said, "Wait. Garrett, let's go to Garrett."

"What's in Garrett?" I asked.

"It doesn't matter," she replied, still semi-frantic. "Let's just go!"

I'd only been to Garrett, Indiana, once before, for some carnival with shitty rides and even shittier funnel cake. It's about twenty miles north of Fort Wayne and has a population of hardly seven thousand (no joke). Suffice it to say that there's even less going on in Garrett than there is in the Fort. So I had absolutely no idea why Emily wanted to go there. She wasn't talking, either, which was beginning to piss me off, seeing as how I rearranged my entire day to accommodate her personal Caspar crisis.

It wasn't until she indicated that Thaddeus should pull into the parking lot of Deb's Dinky Diner that I realized what was going on.

She was trying to make sure we wouldn't see anybody we knew.

I said this to her, almost angrily, but all Em said in return was, "I'll explain inside."

Anyway, it turns out that when Mrs. Whitmarsh heard Caspar say that thing about him and Em sleeping together, she turned into a certified nut job. Not because she's such a prude—at least, I don't think so, because she and Mr. Whitmarsh are always grabbing at each other and stuff—but I'm guessing because she's one of those moms who actually thought her daughter would come to her before doing the deed.

And then, because Mrs. W. couldn't think of any plausible reason why Good Girl Emily would suddenly be behaving in such Bad Girl style, guess who became the scapegoat?

That's right: *me*.

"Wait a minute," I said. "Your mother thinks it's *my* fault that you did it with your boyfriend? What does she think I was doing? Standing by, eating popcorn and coaching you into various positions?"

"It's not rational," Emily admitted. "But the thing is, my mother doesn't have to *be* rational. She's the boss. And now she's saying she doesn't want me seeing you at all—not even at school!"

My first response should've been anger; it's an emotion I know well and am fairly comfortable with. But instead, I just felt sick.

"So it was all lies," I said. "Your mom not hating me? Her caring about my recovery? She was just waiting for an excuse to banish me from your life. It's bad enough she tried to break me and E. up. Now she's hell-bent on taking you away from me too."

Emily didn't say anything, so I didn't either. I sat stonily as a busty blond waitress brought us our coffees.

Ignoring Bianca's audition diet, I asked Busty what kind of pie they had at Deb's Dinky Diner. Then, before she could answer, I said, "Never mind. Bring me one of everything. A la mode."

"Morgan, this sucks," Em said. "And I'm really sorry."

"But . . ." I prompted.

"But what?"

"But whatever," I said bitterly. "You're going to go along

with it. Because, just like your brother, you are incapable of disappointing Mother Whitmarsh."

Emily's eyes narrowed slightly. "That's not fair," she said. "What happened between you and Eli didn't have anything to do with me."

"Right," I said. "Just your mom."

Em sighed. "Look, I'm not going to stop being your friend. I'm here, aren't I? No matter what my mother said."

"Great!" I said brightly. "It's, like, *totally* romantic to have to sneak around just to see your best friend. So tell me: who am I, the Montague or the Capulet?"

I could see that Emily felt terrible about what was going down and that my snarky digs weren't helping her feel any better. But at that moment, I didn't really care how Emily felt.

Why should I, when no one seemed to care how *I* felt?

Ten minutes later, surrounded by slices of apple, blueberry, cherry, strawberry-rhubarb, and pumpkin pie, all of which were drowning in golden-colored vanilla ice cream, I became human again and offered up a sort-of apology.

"It just blows," I said, cramming a forkful of sugary red glaze into my mouth. "One minute your mother adores me and the next I'm the evil temptress. It hurts worse because she should know better. I mean, she *works* with recovering addicts. I'm almost one year sober, you know. I'm a god-damned success story."

Emily said, "I know how hurt you must be. But I really don't think my mom's issue is with you personally. It's what you represent. You know? Like all the photographers at the house and Eli's moodiness—I don't know what's going on with you two, and I don't want to know, either, but he has been hell to live with lately."

This was news to me. Eli, moody? It didn't seem to be in his character. Then again, neither did the whole green-eyed-monster thing.

"I'm going to work on my mother," Emily assured me. "Eli too. In fact, we have a sort-of plan."

"Oh, really?" I said dryly. "Do tell."

Emily grabbed her own fork and stabbed it into the slice of blueberry pie. "We think you should come to church with us tomorrow."

"Church?" I echoed. "No. I don't do God."

"Well, you will," she said. "At least tomorrow. Church is, like, really big with my parents. Attendance isn't an option. Plus, you know, we go out to brunch after services. If you think about it, it's perfect. You'll get brownie points for going to church with us, and then you'll have a chance to make conversation while we eat. Show them that Morgan Carter still has everything they loved about Claudia Miller."

I thought about it for a second, then said, "If your mother has forbidden you to see me, how's she really going to feel about me coming to church with your family?"

"I'm going to tell her it was your idea," she said. "I'm going to tell her you asked me to help you develop your spiritual side."

"In other words," I said, "you're going to lie."

She nodded. "I think you're worth a little sinning."

I pushed the slice of blueberry over to her side of the table. "You and Eli are my best friends," I said. "I never would've survived a week here without you guys. I mean, being Claudia was miserable. Having to be so guarded all the time, worrying that any second the paparazzi could jump out from behind the bushes and ruin everything. Plus, hello?

The fake glasses alone were torture, not to mention the ultra-prissy wardrobe."

Emily chewed thoughtfully for a moment. "It's weird, you know? But that's all part of it. You don't even look like the same person now. You're like . . . I don't know. Like this worldly glamor girl, plunked down in the middle of our boring, average lives."

I could feel frustration building inside me.

"Okay, so maybe I'm not Claudia, but I'm not old-school Morgan anymore either!" I protested. "I'm like . . . like *me*! For the first time. I'm finally getting a chance to figure out who that person is. Or at least I was until this stupid nonsense with Harlan Darly started. And nobody, *nobody* understands what I'm going through."

I flagged Busty for the check, threw down two twenties, and said, "Let's go."

"Aren't you going to wait for change?" Emily asked.

"Screw it," I muttered. "Plenty more where that came from."

Back in the limo, Emily was beyond quiet. I was too, I guess, but more because I was flaming mad. If I opened my mouth, fire might literally shoot out and singe her hair.

Right before we hit Fort Wayne, I said, "So what about Caspar? Are you allowed to see him?"

"Not until I visit my gyno," she replied. "My mother's setting up some kind of scare session about STDs. Like it hasn't been covered in health class."

"Sounds fun," I said.

"Tell me about it." She rolled her eyes.

We were silent again as Thaddeus pulled up to the dog park.

"Okay. I'll go," I told her. "To church, I mean."

"Really?" she said. "Oh, Morgan—thank you! This'll be so good, you'll see."

She hugged me, then put her dark sunglasses back on and sprinted from the limo.

Now I am faced with convincing Bianca that I need to blow off tomorrow's schedule so that I can go to *church*.

Yeah. Like that's not going to sound suspicious. I won't be surprised if Bianca has me followed—just to make sure I'm not actually going to a crack house or something.

But maybe I can spin this somehow—turn it into an opportunity for good press. Tip off a photographer or two?

The Whitmarshes would never guess that the tip came from me. After all, they're being stalked in their own home, right?

Church or no church, I don't have a chance in hell of winning these people over.

11/20—*Much, much later*

Came home to an empty house. Trudy left a note saying she's spending the night at Dave's but I should give her a ring if I need anything. I felt too stupid to call just to tell her I needed a hug, so I jumped into the shower and tried to make the anger and hurt wash off in the tub.

The phone rang around ten, and I was practically doing cartwheels when I heard Marissa's voice on the other end of the line. She told me all about her time in the Russian tundra and what it was like to make out with Ewan McGregor ("Perfect." She sighed. "Slightly moist and just a little bit firm. I didn't even mind when he slipped me some tongue.") It gave me a bit of a pang—not the part about Ewan but the part

112

about Marissa making movies while I'm stuck here, cast as the town harlot and auditioning for *Okla*-freaking-*homa!*

Then she asked about how I was doing, and I didn't want to tell her at first, but she'd already gotten the e-mail about Eli's and my disastro-date. So I filled her in on Emily and how Mother Whitmarsh was ready to put out a restraining order to keep me from her kids. I even told her about the humiliating incident with Debbie Ackerman back at the salon.

"Morgan!" she admonished. "When are you going to teach that girl a lesson? Seriously, this is so not like you."

"I know!" I said. "I'm off my game!"

We spent the next hour or so planning Operation Screw Debbie or, as I like to refer to it, OSD. Here's what we came up with:

Phase I:

Land lead in school play. Do not gloat, as D.A. will be expecting this. Instead, kill with kindness.

Phase II:

"Redecorate" D.A.'s ill-gotten Jetta. Write nasty message on windshield with shoe polish, "paint" exterior in Silly String, tie cans of Spam to rear bumper. As long as no permanent damage is done, "redecoration" will be viewed as a prank. Establish alibi ahead of time so as not to have culpability.

Phase III:

Convince Riley to help out by "wooing" D.A. and letting her think he's into her. Have him invite her to Winter Wonderdance, then stand her up. If she confronts him, have him publicly deny ever asking her. She will be humiliated!

That last one was Marissa's idea, and when I suggested it might be a bit too mean, she said, "Do not forget that this girl *sold you out*. And then used the money to buy a brand-new car. And continues to talk to you like you are scum on her shoe. She deserves a whole lot more mean than *this*."

"Maybe this is stupid," I said with a sigh. "I thought things were good here, but maybe I should just . . . you know. Pack up and come home."

I expected Marissa to squeal an affirmative, "Yes, finally!" When she didn't, I said, "Are you honestly going to tell me I'm better off in Fort Lame?"

It took her a minute to answer, so I knew she was choosing her words carefully. "It's not that," she said slowly. "I'm just wondering—what if things were peachy keen with Farm Boy and his mama? Would you still be talking about coming back to Cali?"

"Of course," I said indignantly, but I knew it was a lie even as I said it. "What's your point?"

"Not to sound too Sandy Cohen or anything, but running away from your problems doesn't mean you leave them behind, you know?"

I felt like dropping the f-bomb on her but decided against it. Mostly because I knew she was right.

"Fine," I snapped. "You do sound like Sandy Cohen, though."

"Look," she said, "I gotta get going. Hot date—and no, I can't tell you who with because I swear the *Enquirer* has a tap on my cell phone. You *are* listening, aren't you, you insidious assholes? Go write about some alien abduction already, will you?"

To me, she said, "Fax your flight info to my assistant

tomorrow and I will personally pick you up at LAX next Wednesday. Okay? You can even crash at my place if you want. I've got, like, four guest bedrooms. No, wait—five. Four? Shit, I can't even remember!"

I laughed. Marissa works so steadily she's hardly ever home for more than a few weeks. No wonder she couldn't remember how many rooms the decorator had designated for guests.

"Fine," I said, "you've got yourself a deal." We air-kissed into the phone and said our "I love yous," and for a second, I felt like maybe everything would be okay. I had one more day of Broadway Boot Camp to get through before auditions on Monday and then another forty hours before I'd be boarding a plane to Los Angeles. I'd been dreading spending Thanksgiving with the Travoltas, but I'd fully forgotten that I'd have four other days to do whatever I want, with whomever I want. Namely, Marissa.

Off to bed now.

11/21

Holy shite! In the few days I've been working with Fabrizio, I actually dropped a full six pounds. He says it's mostly water weight, but that's 'cause I lied and told him I gave up the caffeine cold turkey (I haven't). I think I'm going to ask Bianca if I can keep working with him three times a week, because I bet I could have the beginnings of a six-pack in another month or two.

Must go put on final coat of lip gloss before the twins arrive for our church date.

Well, I tried. Nobody can say I didn't try.

Yet it was still a total disaster.

I had the costume down pat. I'd pulled my hair into a Peggy Sue ponytail and put on a tailored, just-above-the-knee-length wool skirt in gray, a black turtleneck sweater, black tights, and black Mary Janes. I even wore the pearls Bianca gave me on my thirteenth birthday—stud earrings and a sixteen-inch graduated necklace with a platinum and-diamond clasp. As a final touch, I wrapped the elastic of my ponytail with a gray tweed scrunchie I found in the bath-room (I didn't think Trudy would mind) and painted on sev-eral coats of ballerina pink lip gloss.

Eli rang the doorbell a good five minutes earlier than we'd agreed on, but it was okay because I'd been ready for at least an hour. He was fidgeting as I opened the door—bouncing one knee and chewing on the corner of his thumb. I'd never seen him do either before today.

"What's wrong?" I asked, the alarm in my voice so intense even *I* flinched.

"I'll tell you in the car," he said. "Oh, and you look . . . nice."

Was the "nice" some sort of euphemism? Or was he being sincere? My head felt heavy and hot, and a few beads of sweat squeezed out from behind my neck. It was twenty degrees outside, but under my ribbed turtleneck sweater, the temperature had shot up to a hundred and twenty.

In the car, I said, "You did tell your parents I was coming, right?"

Eli nodded.

"Let me guess," I continued. "They're not happy about it."

This time, Eli said nothing.

"So why didn't you just cancel it?" I asked.

"Truth?" he asked. "Emily wouldn't let me."

"Oh, that's swell," I said. "Because I so enjoy being thrust into awkward social situations with people who hate my guts. What were the two of you *thinking*?"

His eyebrows knit themselves together tightly, like he was concentrating on a physics equation. Then Eli eased the Taurus off the road and into an unfamiliar neighborhood. "Let's skip it," he said.

"Church?"

"Yes, church. And brunch. Let's skip it all and go do something else entirely."

He was wearing nice tan pants with creases ironed in, a white dress shirt, and a chocolate–and–robin's-egg-blue-colored tie.

"Like what?" I said, indicating his outfit. "Crash a wedding? Besides," I went on, "I don't think your mother would much appreciate me being the cause of you skipping church. Then I wouldn't just be an ex-addict and a whore, I'd also be a heretic. No thanks!"

"It's too hard, Morgan," Eli said, and my throat felt like it was closing up.

Here it was. The big kiss-off. The permanent one I'd been fearing since I first realized that I liked Eli to begin with.

"What's too hard?" I asked, trying to swallow my fear.

"Trying to make everybody happy!" he said, and I wasn't sure if that included me.

But then he said, "We like each other, right? So that's all that matters. Who cares what my mother thinks? What's she going to do, have me followed twenty-four-seven? No. So screw what she thinks. Screw *her*!"

I could tell it took a lot for Eli to add that last "screw," especially in relation to his mother. For a minute I thought, *Hmmm, maybe I am a bad influence on Eli.* But then I thought, no. It's good that he's learning how to stand up to his mom. Because otherwise, she'd just end up running his life. No one would ever be good enough, even if he found some younger version of her (with different DNA, of course).

"Okay, then," I said. "We'll go to church."

Eli looked at me, his face scrunched up in confusion.

I sighed.

"Look, if you really want to give your mom's judgment the finger, the best way to do it is for us to show up and act like we don't give a damn what she thinks. I'll be sweet, and you'll be respectful, and after a while, she's going to have to get the hint that we're the ones who call the shots, not her."

He grinned. "See? You *are* more experienced than me."

He pulled back onto the road, and five minutes later, we were squeezing into the packed parking lot of Trinity Presbyterian Church. When we entered the chapel, Emily was standing guard by the door. She led us to the pew where the Whitmarsh parents were seated.

Mrs. Whitmarsh was looking at her watch. When she saw us, she glanced up and said, "Oh. Good. You made it."

That was all. No hellos, no nice-to-see-yous, nothing.

Mrs. W. scooted down far enough so that Emily and Eli could fit next to her. I, however, didn't have a seat—unless Eli's lap counted as an option.

Emily whispered, "Mom—we need more room."

"But this is where I always sit," she replied primly.

Em turned to Eli and rolled her eyes, then gently elbowed

her mother into moving farther down. Even so, I barely had enough pew space to squeeze my butt between Eli and the wooden side rail. So I turned to him and said, "I didn't know it was kosher to sit this close together in church."

Eli chuckled and I grinned; Mrs. Whitmarsh pushed Mr. Whitmarsh way farther down the pew and urged the rest of us to spread out more.

Mission accomplished.

The service was nice enough: there was a decent choir accompanied by an even more decent organist. The pastor was an enormously fat man who looked like the mom from *Hairspray*, had the guy playing her not been in drag. His hair was a mess of silvery-white curls, and he had at least three chins. But I was still pretty open to him—until he started this week's sermon, which was devoted to Exodus 20:12— "Honor your father and your mother, that your days may be long in the land which the Lord your God gives you."

I closed my eyes and gave my head a little shake. Of all the verses in the Bible, *this* was the one Pastor Boyd had to choose? Today of all days?

To get through it, I tuned out the sermon and did what I always do when I'm bored and need to stay awake: I started running through Billy Joel lyrics in my head. Don't ask me why, but I can't tell you how many times I've saved my own ass with "Scenes from an Italian Restaurant" or even "We Didn't Start the Fire." Because when you run lyrics in your head, especially complicated ones, you look like you're really concentrating on what the other person has to say.

It's especially effective in meetings with Harvey Weinstein.

When it was over, a lot of people flocked to Mr. and Mrs.

Whitmarsh. I could see how they'd be popular in the church, what with his political position and her ties to the community. They were good-looking, God-fearing people with a fine set of twins.

But it didn't take long to realize that the real draw was *me*.

I guess it was a big deal, me coming to Trinity Presbyterian. Out of all the churches in Fort Wayne—and there was one on every corner, way more than there were 7-Elevens or Exxon stations—I'd come to theirs. The regulars, the ones who knew the Whitmarshes, looked tickled that they'd somehow convinced me to choose this church over all others.

So the next twenty or thirty minutes was spent pressing the flesh with a myriad of people asking the Whitmarshes for an introduction. I kept a serene smile pasted on my face and kept saying things like, "Lovely sermon, wasn't it?" and, "The choir was amazing today, weren't they?" I knew that E. and Em would think I sounded like a big phony, but I was hoping the performance would elevate my status in Mrs. W.'s eyes.

Yes, I know what I'd said to Eli. It didn't mean that I stopped wishing the woman would like me again.

Anyway, it didn't work. She just kept giving me the up-down and asking me things like, "Morgan, do you have a cold? Your eyes look awfully *red*," and then pointedly staring at her husband. I could read the cartoon bubble over her head: *Look, honey, our son is dating a crack whore.*

But the proverbial shit hit the fan over breakfast at Cindy's. Or rather, waiting to be seated for breakfast at Cindy's. The diner is set in this smallish Airstream trailer, so when you have to wait for a table, you do it outside. Mrs. Whitmarsh, who'd put our name in when we arrived, was getting more and more impatient. She wouldn't come right out and say it, though. No, she would just jiggle her foot, look at her watch, and say things along the lines of, "I wonder why it's so busy today. Oh, right, we usually arrive half an hour earlier."

Instead of letting her get to me, I excused myself to use the ladies' room. I didn't actually need to use the bathroom, though. I knew from past experience that if *I* was the one requesting the table, there'd be no wait. Sure enough, I'd barely made it out the door and into the waiting line before the hostess called out, "Carter, party of five?"

Carter, as opposed to Whitmarsh, so my secret good deed wasn't a secret anymore. Within a minute, the Whitmarshes and I were seated at a large table in the back, bused so perfectly that the Formica tabletop literally gleamed.

I figured I should just own up to what I'd done, so I said, "See? Being a celebrity has *some* perks."

I expected to get a little giggle out of everyone—or at the very least, Eli—but instead, Mr. and Mrs. Whitmarsh exchanged worried glances for, like, the seventeenth time this morning.

So I tucked my napkin into my lap and vowed not to speak unless spoken to.

After the waitress had brought our drinks—OJ for Eli and Em, herbal tea for Mr. and Mrs. Whitmarsh, and coffee for me—Mrs. W. said, "Morgan, I hear you're headed to California for Thanksgiving."

"Yes," I said, a little too enthusiastically. "We're having dinner at the Travoltas' house. My mother is, like, way stoked. I don't think she's cooked a turkey in her entire life. She always manages to wrangle us an invite to someone else's lavishly catered dinner."

"I see," she said. A strained smile played on her lips.

"It kind of sucks," I babbled on. "I was really hoping my parents would come out here so we could have, you know, the whole Stove Top experience. A real down-home kind of thing."

"Down-home kind of thing," Mrs. W. repeated.

Trying to redeem myself, I continued, "What I mean is . . . you know. I wanted a real Thanksgiving. With my family. And turkey. And Stove Top. And, like, that stupid parade on the TV and touch football in the backyard. I never had any of that growing up, so . . ."

Maybe I imagined it, but for a second, I thought I saw Mrs. Whitmarsh's face soften just a bit.

If I'd stopped there, things might have smoothed themselves out. Instead, my big mouth didn't know when to quit.

"Hey," I said, "it won't be all bad. I'll get to raid my closet and bring back some decent clothes, and if I play my cards just right, I can probably convince my mother that I need to get my highlights redone at Louis Licari. Plus, I'll get to fly first class, and I haven't done that in, like, almost a *year*."

You know how sometimes you're talking and you don't realize how what you're saying sounds until it's too late?

Yeah. That was me.

There's more, but sadly, the above constitutes the bright spots of my morning.

Later, after the Breakfast of Doom had ended and Mrs. Whitmarsh told E. and Em to be home within the hour, the twins and I headed to my house to deconstruct.

"It's just that . . ." Em began. "Well, you kind of caused a stir at church."

"But I didn't do anything!" I said. "I didn't even sing the hymns!"

"What Em means," Eli clarified, "is that Mom and Dad are pretty serious about church. So when, you know, it turned into an autograph session? My guess is that Mom thought that was kind of disrespectful to the Lord."

"Your mom's got issues," I grumbled.

"Oh, please," Emily said. "That could've been so much worse."

I couldn't see how, but she and Eli said in unison, "Trust me."

To change the subject, I asked Em how things were going with Caspar, and she said we'd talk about it later. Then she asked me if I was really dreading my trip back to California, and I said we'd talk about it later, and then Eli goes, "How did *I* end up the third wheel here?" So then we tried to make conversation that included Eli.

He surprised me when he said, "I keep meaning to tell you, I thought of a good one."

"A good one what?" I asked.

"Who's that chick that Tom Cruise used to date?"

"Katie Holmes?" I offered.

He shook his head. "No, the one before her. The Spanish one."

"Oh, you mean Penelope Cruz."

"Right. Her." He grinned. "Penelope Cruz is the poor man's Frida Kahlo."

It took me a minute to realize that he meant Selma Hayek, but when I figured it out, I couldn't have been more proud.

"That *is* a good one," I said. "Marissa's going to love it."

All in all, the second half of the morning was pretty good, and for a few minutes, it felt like everything had gone back to normal, whatever that means.

It's only three in the afternoon, but I feel drunk with exhaustion. Nap time!

11/22

Debbie Ackerman is going *down.*

Up until this point, Debs had been more of an annoyance than anything else. Sure, I was PO'd that she was spreading rumors about me, and I hated her cocky "I'm so much better than you because I'm corn-fed and you're an ex-addict" attitude. Not to mention how she flaunts that car of hers and how she keeps trying to snuggle up to my sort-of boyfriend.

Even so, I'd managed to keep a relatively good sense of humor about the whole "feud."

Until this morning, that is, when the front page of the Fort Wayne *Journal Gazette* read, "HOLLYWOOD STARLET SETS SIGHTS ON LEAD IN SNIDER H.S. SPRING MUSICAL."

The story went on to talk about all the lessons Bianca set up for me, right down to the salad-and-bottled-water diet I was supposed to be following. I kid you not. Debbie Ackerman actually called a reporter, and this reporter and his editors thought this little item was so newsworthy they spent all of yesterday chasing down corroborating facts about Bianca's Boot Camp. Even Fabrizio affirmed that I was seeing him to "firm up some flab."

The only one who didn't sell me out? Thaddeus, who's still quoted in the article but as saying, "No comment." Too bad he didn't bother to comment to *me*, because it would've been nice to have a heads-up on this, the latest of my humiliations.

"Don't listen to those losers," Delia said to me, gesturing to just about everyone in the cafeteria. "They're just jealous because you're a *professional*. And don't you worry—Debbie Ackerman will eat it when you land the lead and she ends up in the chorus."

That's one thing you've got to love about Delia. No matter what happens, she's always this big ball of positive energy. At least, when it comes to me, she is.

I decided it was high time to fill everybody in on Operation Screw Debbie. Delia squealed with delight as I explained each phase, but everyone else at our table—including Riley—looked uncomfortable. I steeled myself, waiting for their response, but nobody was saying anything.

So finally, I said, "Are you guys going to help me or what?"

"I'm so in," Delia said. "The squad's ready to back me up. In fact, why don't you leave phase two to us? No one would ever guess that we'd be involved."

"Excellent!" I said. Then I turned to Riley. "What about you?"

But before he could say anything, Eli jumps in with this: "Why didn't you ask me?"

"What do you mean?" I said. "Ask you what?"

"Why do you want *him* to woo Debbie?" Eli said, with a dismissive flip of his hand. "I mean, *I'm* the one she's in love with, remember?"

"Um, Eli?" I said. "Now's not the time for jealousy, okay? We've got some serious business to take care of."

"Jealousy?" Eli replied tightly. "You think I'm *jealous*?"

I leaned into him and, keeping my voice low, I said, "Maybe I don't want you wooing Debbie because . . . because . . . maybe *I'm* jealous."

It was total bullshit, and Eli called me on it immediately.

"Come on, Morgan. It makes the most sense for me to do it. Don't you see? She'll be even more humiliated when she finds out it's you who I actually took to the Winter Wonderdance."

"Eli!" Emily exclaimed. "What the hell is wrong with you?"

"What?" he said.

Em shook her head. "I don't like this. You're acting like a big fat jerk."

"Excuse me," I cut in. "This was *my* plan, remember?"

"I'd expect it from you," she said. "But don't drag my brother into your sordid scheme, okay?"

"Expect it from me?" I repeated. "Why, because *I* am a big fat jerk? Are you forgetting everything this girl did to me?"

"No," she said testily. "But it's not nice to crush people who are weaker than you. And don't forget that until this all went down, Debbie was one of my best friends. I sided with you. *Everyone* sided with you. But trust me, Debbie's miserable inside—I don't care how tough she's acting."

She rose with her tray. "So don't forget that," she finished, directing the words more to Eli than me. Then she got up from the table and walked away without another word.

"Fine," Eli said. Then again: "Fine!"

127

"Yo, chill out, dude," Riley said. "Don't be such a spaz."

I winced. Sore spot. To say the least.

Eli's face turned purple. Then he goes, "You know what? Emily's right. I don't need to get involved with this. Let Riley do your dirty work for you. And when he's done? Maybe he can take you to the dance."

And then he stormed off as well.

I sat there, staring after them. What had just happened?

Riley said, "So, you ready for the big audition?"

"What?" I asked absently.

"Landing the lead *is* phase one, right?" Riley shrugged. "I don't see how I can help you with phase three if there's no phase one."

I focused my attention. "Wait—so *you'll* help me?" I asked.

"You knew I would," he shot back.

Then Delia said, "Don't let Emily get to you. She's always been such a goody-goody. And Eli will cool off. That boy adores you."

"Right," I said, wishing I sounded more convincing.

Now Ms. Bowman is positively *beaming* at me, and I have about two whole minutes until the final bell rings. Then I have about fifteen minutes to find a nice quiet place to run my sirens and other assorted vocal exercises before what ironically could turn out to be the most important audition of my life. I wouldn't be surprised if those sleaze-balls at the *Journal Gazette* actually sent a reporter over to cover tryouts. Thank God that bastard Fabrizio did knock those six pounds off my gut or I'd be even more of a nervous wreck right now.

AUDITIONS FOR SNIDER HIGH SCHOOL'S SPRING PRODUC-
TION OF *OKLAHOMA!*

SCENE 1 — Snider High Auditorium

Roughly forty-five high schoolers litter the stage as an overenthusiastic high school drama teacher who's a few cards short of a deck (MS. BOWMAN) tries to make them sit in one enormous circle. As she does this, the auditorium seating fills up with curious students and teachers (including some from different schools!), not to mention reporters and photographers from both the Journal Gazette AND its rival, the News-Sentinel. Our reluctant heroine, MORGAN CARTER, sits sandwiched between the bubble-headed DELIA and a hotter-than-normal RILEY.

MORGAN (to Delia): Besides the hacks, who are all these people? Better question: why are they *here*?

Riley laughs, causing Morgan to turn and face him. She wears a slight frown.

MORGAN: What's so funny?

RILEY: I always find it amusing when someone asks a question they already know the answer to. Or worse, where there's a particular answer they're looking for. Like, "Honey, do these jeans make me look like fat?" The only acceptable answer to that question, even if the girl asking it is three hundred pounds, isn't, "No." It's, "You are not fat." Any variation and you're in the doghouse for weeks. Anyway, what were you saying? Oh, right, you were pretending you didn't know why all these people are here.

MORGAN: I wasn't *pretending* anything.

RILEY: Let's ask Delia. Delia, do you think Morgan honestly doesn't know why all of these people are packed into the Snider High auditorium on this particular day?

DELIA: Um . . .

RILEY (to Morgan): The answer is you, toots.

MORGAN: Me what?

RILEY: *You* you. You, toots, are the reason for all of this.

MORGAN: Did you just call me "toots"? Twice?

129

RILEY: Shhh. I think we're about to start.

SCENE 2 — The Music Room

The students have now been divided into three groups. Group A is on the stage, doing touchy-feely acting exercises complete with trust challenges. Group B is in the gym, which is behind the auditorium — hence the perpetual sweaty gym sock smell of said auditorium — learning a quick dance routine. Reporters and other onlookers have been banned from this area as well as the music room, where group C is finishing a round of vocal warm-ups before they begin to sing the solo pieces they've prepared. Morgan is infinitely grateful that there will be no reporters and/or photographers allowed into either the gym or the music room, as she's tired of having her private humiliations made public.

Okay, abandoning the script format for this scene because I think there's absolutely no way I could possibly capture the hilarity that ensued.

First there was the thing with Mrs. Allen. She's the oldest of the three music teachers, as well as the crustiest and most conservative. So conservative, in fact, that she was worried *Oklahoma!* was too racy for Snider High because what kind of message does Ado Annie, Laurey's slutty friend and a good source of the show's comic relief, send to young girls? (Clearly, she's never tuned into an episode of *Laguna Beach*, or she'd realize how positively G-rated Annie is, comparatively.)

Anyway, you can only begin to imagine how pleased Allen was when Meadow Forrester and Colin McAfee told her they intended to perform their audition piece together, singing—and this is so classic—"The Internet Is for Porn," from *Avenue Q.*

"Oh, for goodness' sake!" Mrs. Allen scoffed. "I hardly think some *rap* song is appropriate."

"But it's not a rap song," Meadow said, all indignant. "It's from a Tony Award–winning play!" She handed her the book of sheet music. "See?"

Mrs. Allen slid her reading glasses to the tippity tip of her nose. Everyone in group C watched as she combed the lines. I'm not sure which was funnier—watching Mrs. Allen's eyes bug out when she hit the line about masturbation or realizing that Meadow was totally serious about using it.

Finally, Mrs. Allen sighed and said, "Just to the end of the first verse. That's all."

Meadow looked crestfallen over this news, but Colin whispered something in her ear that restored the bright smile to her face. That Colin. I bet he's the one who convinced her that a song about double-clicking a certain unmentionable body part was perfect for their audition.

My vocal coach and I had argued over what I should sing because Bianca's right—singing really isn't my forte. But I can carry a decent tune if it's in the right range. Typically, *Oklahoma!*'s Laurey is an extreme soprano—think Mariah Carey breaking glass—but that's so far out of my league I can't even *see* the league it's in.

Veronique wanted me to do "Send in the Clowns," but I told her that clowns freak me out so badly that I couldn't even sing about them. At one point, she had me doing "Don't Cry for Me, Argentina," but all I could think was, *Yeah, that'll help my prima donna image.*

As far as Veronique knows, we agreed that I'd sing "I Feel Pretty" from *West Side Story*—a safe, solid song just a tad too high for my limited voice. But V. had worked me pretty

131

hard with all the hissing and nose-humming and scales and stuff, so in the end I probably wouldn't sound half bad.

Even so, the song was never really me, so secretly I'd been practicing "Frank Mills," from *Hair*. I like it because it's short and sweet, it's in my vocal range, and it has the added benefit of making me sound just a little bit vulnerable, which I've figured out is key to the character of Laurey.

So I got up and I warbled my song, and right on the line "Tell him Angela and I don't want the two dollars back—just him," my eyes filled up with tears. Just like that, totally unexpectedly.

I'd like to say it was because I was feeling the poignancy of the song—or it was my acting chops kicking in—but really, it had nothing to do with either. It was like suddenly I could feel him in the room—Eli, I mean—and when I looked up, he actually *was* standing in the doorway, camera in hand, *click click clicking* the shutter. I sucked in a deep breath that sounded a bit like a gasp, and he disappeared before I could even give him a little wave.

Anyway, I'd assumed that after that, we'd be given sides to read, but instead of passing out scenes or monologues, Ms. Bowman led us through a series of bizarre exercises— the kind that acting teachers love to assign but that are totally useless in the real world.

MS. B: Morgan. Imagine, if you will, that you're a cat.

ME: A cat? What kind of cat?

MS. B: Domesticated.

ME: I don't understand.

MS. B: Domesticated. Like a pet.

ME: Yes, I know what *domesticated* means.

MS. B: So, then, be a domesticated cat!

ME (deadpan): But what's my motivation?

MS. B (missing the point of my sarcasm): You are a striped tabby cat hoping to take a luxurious nap in the sun.

And so on.

After we were dismissed, Riley came up to me and asked me if I wanted a ride home. I told him I already had one.

"Oh, right," he said. "I forgot about your limo."

I said, "Believe me—I'd much rather a different mode of transportation. I mean, Thaddeus is great and all, but it's kind of hard to blend in when your ride is a chauffeured town car."

Callbacks are tomorrow, and then I'm ditching school on Wednesday to fly out to California. I wish Trudy were going with me, but Dave asked her to Thanksgiving dinner at his parents' house, and this is a sort of big step for them in terms of couplehood. I mean, they've only been dating like three or four months

Once upon a time I thought (hoped?) that Eli would've wanted me at his family's Thanksgiving dinner. I even sort of pictured Bianca and Sam joining us in Fort Wayne for one of those Norman Rockwell kind of holidays.

Fat chance. At this point, at the rate I'm going, Mr. and Mrs. John Travolta will turn out to be vegetarians, and I'll spend the day pretending to enjoy choking down lumps of Tofurky with organic mushroom gravy. (NOTE TO SELF: Go on Google and see if Scientologists are down with meat.)

Truth be told, though, I'm a little relieved to be getting a break from this place.

Fort Wayne has totally been testing my patience these

days. And maybe—well, maybe right now L.A. feels a bit more like where I belong.

Not that I would *ever* tell Bianca that. Or Eli. Or even Em.

As Sam would say, "More anon."

11/23

No. *No*. This can't be happening.

I just checked the callback list that Ms. Bowman posted and *get this*: Debbie "Pontius Pilate" Ackerman is *on it*. Her name is right next to mine. For the role of *Laurey*, no less.

I really didn't need this today. Not today, when the morning papers carried inane stories about yesterday's audition, down to what I was wearing(!) and how I seemed to be flirting with a fellow student (I'm sure Mrs. Whitmarsh celebrated with a round of mimosas when she read that). Plus, I'd made up my mind to try and patch things up with Eli before I leave for California. And because lunch is too short a period to have a decent conversation—not to mention the complete lack of privacy the caf affords—I was planning on doing it *after* callbacks, not before.

Where are Ms. Janet Moore and her M&M-laced therapy when you need them?

11/23—*Later*

It's almost midnight and I'm still not packed and Thaddeus is picking me up at 4:30 a.m. (EST) because Bianca scheduled the first leg of my flight at some ungodly hour that puts me in L.A. by 7:45 a.m. (PST). This is the same woman who considers a 10 a.m. wakeup call an "early day." Marissa phoned a few hours ago to get my flight info because I forgot to fax it like she asked, and when I told her my arrival time, she informed me that I better make sure I have plenty of Starbucks money on me because I'm going to have to buy her a gallon of espresso just so she'll be conscious enough to drive me home.

At first, she asked me if she could send Dotti, her brain-less, bra-less assistant, to pick me up instead. I think she expected me to say, "No problem," because the old, always-stoned version of me probably would've said that. But I gently reminded her that Dotti's cousin, who was married to a shady "diet doctor," had once been my amphetamine connection, and she begrudgingly agreed to drive herself and give Dotti the morning off.

Anyway.

I've spent the last hour sitting in the middle of my bedroom, sobbing. This is a rerun of the two other crying jags I had earlier in the evening. The first took place during dinner—Trudy and I had ordered in Chinese, but the dude who took our order gave me kung pao chicken instead of kung pao beef, and this was enough to send me over the edge. Trudy asked me what was wrong, but all I could say was, "I don't want the chicken!"

Then she made me a cup of Tension Tamer tea and I calmed down long enough for *her* to tell *me* what was really wrong.

"You're nervous about going back to L.A.," she said gently, stirring Splenda into my teacup. "So much has changed since you left three months ago, not the least of which is *you*."

The second crying jag was interpreted by Marissa, who hypothesized that I was a mess because I didn't have any sort of closure with Eli. This made me panic even harder.

"I don't want *closure*!" I informed her. "*Closure* implies an ending!"

She sighed. "Look, hon," she said. "Don't shoot the messenger, okay? But you and Eli were never going to work out. You're, like, a million years ahead of him. Why do you think I'm forced to date older men?"

"Because your shit-head father ran out on you when you were five and as a result you developed an overly pronounced daddy complex?" I guessed, sniffing.

"*Right*," she replied without missing a beat. "It wouldn't have anything to do with me joining the workforce at age two, would it?"

I said, "You don't get it. That's partly what I liked so much about Eli. He was normal. Kind of nerdy, but supersmart, and super-sweet, and super-into-me."

"Ah, but there's your flaw in logic," she said. "He wasn't into *you* for very long. It was *Claudia* he courted, remember? He ditched *you* the day after the *Oprah* thing. I imagine the kid just about shat his pants. Like he woke up suddenly and said, 'Holy crap! How did *I* end up dating a movie star?'"

"He didn't ditch me," I said. "We got back together, remember?"

"Yet you keep breaking up," she reminded me gently.

After we got off the phone, I started to regret not catching up with Eli, as I'd originally planned, because maybe Marissa was right—maybe everything felt a little too undone. So I tried to call Eli's cell, but he didn't pick up.

So that brought me to here—"here" meaning way after midnight and still not packed and on the cusp of yet another crying jag. What is *wrong* with me? Maybe while I'm home,

I'll stop in and see Dr. Gildea, get a prescription for antidepressants or something.

Can I even take antidepressants? I don't know. *I don't know.*

Crap—is there someone at the *door*?

11/24—*Ridiculously early in the morning*

I don't even know where to begin.

Let's just say that I'm flying, and the plane hasn't even taken off the ground.

Wait—that sounds bad, like I've taken some pills or something. I haven't. Swear to God. The only thing I'm high on is L-O-V-E.

Er, maybe we should call it "deeply intense like with much potential for true love."

But I'm getting ahead of myself. Let me back up a bit.

So, there really *was* someone at the door.

Eli.

"You rang?" he said, clearly trying to look casual even though his cheeks were flushed from the cold.

I didn't know how to respond, so I didn't. I just stared at him. He was wearing flannel pajama bottoms in red-and-navy-blue plaid, a Snider High sweatshirt over a T-shirt, and a puffy dark green jacket that was left unzipped. He had total bed head, not to mention those pinky British-boy cheeks, and even though I felt like I'd just swallowed a sparrow, I could already see how this had the makings of a very romantic scene. All that was missing was a boom box hoisted high over his head. That and the kind of fake, driving rain that makes people declare their love for one another.

You know, like in just about every John Cusack film ever made.

Eli asked, "You mind if I come in? I'm kind of freezing my ass off."

"Ass" is not a word I've heard escape Eli's lips often—if ever. The only thing that would've left me more stunned was if he'd said "balls."

Anyway, he came in. Then he just stood there, and his mouth was twisted in this way that made it look like he had a million words he was waiting to spill. But he didn't say anything.

Finally, I said, "What are you doing here? At, like, one in the morning?"

He nodded vigorously, like, "Yes, I agree, that's a valid question." But still he said nothing.

"Well?" I prompted.

"I would've been here earlier but I had to, you know, wait. Until my parents were asleep."

ME: Yes, but why?

ELI: You called my cell.

ME: But you didn't pick up.

ELI: I know.

ME: So how did you know it wasn't an accident? The call, I mean.

ELI: I didn't.

ME: You're telling me you snuck out of your house and drove all the way over here because you thought I *might* have wanted to talk to you?

ELI: Well . . .

ME: There has to be another reason. Right? Go on. Spill it.

ELI:

ME (sighing): Look, Eli—if you're not going to say anything, you should probably go. I still have to pack, and I have this ridiculously early flight —

ELI: No.

ME: No?

ELI: There's something I want to say. I just need a minute, okay?

ME: Yeah, okay.

This is when the sparrow-in-the-stomach feeling got even stronger. It reminded me of how I felt the first time I rode the Boomerang at Knott's Berry Farm. I don't know if it was because I was overtired, or if it was because Eli showed up at my door in the middle of the night, or if was because he refused to take his eyes off me and his unfaltering gaze was fully intense.

Eli shrugged out of his jacket and draped it on the back of a dining room chair. "You want me to make some coffee?" he asked. "Both of the Starbucks I went to closed at eleven."

I said, "You stopped to bring me coffee?"

He nodded. "It is, as you've already pointed out, one in the morning."

"Right," I said.

I followed him into the kitchen and watched as he put the paper filter into the basket, carefully poured out eight heaping scoops of extra-dark French roast, and filled up the water tank using the Brita pitcher from the fridge. As the machine started to hiss and pop, I said, "I'm leaving for L.A. tomorrow."

"I know," he said. "Emily told me."

Then I said, "I don't know if I'm ever coming back."

It wasn't true—at least, I hadn't been thinking of this trip as a one-way sort of deal. Had I?

I mean, if I hadn't planned on returning—even subconsciously—then why had I tried out for the school play?

Why hadn't I packed a single thing in the cheap vinyl suit-case I arrived with three months ago?

I hadn't said it as a test, either. Like, I wasn't *trying* to make Eli's face take on that wide-eyed, semi-slack-jawed shape. But secretly I enjoyed the shocked look my statement had caused.

"Actually," I said, picking up my coffee and taking a small sip, "that isn't true. I *am* coming back. I don't know why I just said that. I'm sorry."

Eli sighed—out of relief? Frustration? Exhaustion?

Then: silence.

After a long, long pause, Eli said slowly, "I'm glad you're coming back."

"Me too," I replied.

Back to dialogue for a sec—

ELI: But even if you weren't, I'd still need to do this.

ME: Do what?

ELI: Apologize.

ME: For . . . ?

ELI: A lot.

ME: Like . . . ?

ELI: I'm the one who keeps screwing up things between us.

ME:

ELI: I should never have blindsided you at Casa's that night.

ME:

ELI: And I shouldn't have been acting like a jealous brat just because you're friends with that . . . that Riley.

ME:

ELI: And I shouldn't have used my mother as an excuse to slow things down between us when really, she had nothing to do with it.

ME: Wait a minute—are you telling me your mother *doesn't* hate me?

ELI: No, she hates you. But if I hadn't needed an out, I never would've let her get in the way.

ME: Oh, really? I hadn't realized you were looking for an out.

ELI: Let me explain. Think back to when you first met me. Remember how you thought I was just this weird, lame dork?

ME: I never said—

ELI (interrupting me): You didn't have to. I could see it in the way you looked at me. And then something happened—I don't know what, but something—and it was like I was a different person to you. Everything changed, even the sound of your voice when you talked to me. It was slower, less impatient. I could see you listening to whatever I said instead of just pretending to listen.

ME:

ELI: Anyway, I think that's what happened with you. Like, one minute you're just the new girl from Lancaster, Pennsylvania, and you're cute and you're sharp and you don't take crap from anyone, but you're still really soft and vulnerable. And then suddenly you're not you anymore, and I have to figure out the truths from the lies, and before you remind me how many times you've apologized for all that, let me just say that I know you're sorry, but you being sorry didn't make it any easier for me to understand. Do you get what I'm trying to say?

ME:

ELI: Nod once for yes, twice for no.

ME (nodding once):

ELI: Good. Okay. So, there I was, trying to sort it all out, and there were, like, cameras everywhere, and junk journalists calling the house every five seconds, and you didn't have your glasses anymore, and you dyed your hair red and started wearing perfume and shiny lip gloss. . . . You didn't look the same or smell the same or taste the same—

ME: And you got spooked.

ELI: Yes. I did.

ME: I can't believe the bitch was right.

ELI: Excuse me?

ME: Marissa. She called it exactly. She said that you preferred Claudia to Morgan—to *me*—and that once you realized who I was . . . who I used to be . . . your feelings changed.

ELI: But no. *No.* My feelings haven't changed. I'm just having trouble figuring out what to do with them. I mean, my mom's yapping in my ear that this is all just a publicity stunt and that you probably won't finish out the marking period, let alone the whole school year. And then I see you with that . . . that *Riley* . . . and he's older and better-looking and way cooler than me. And you guys have that whole theater thing in common.

ME: Yet you're the only boy I make out with on a consistent basis. Or any basis, for that matter.

I drained my cup of coffee and sat there as Eli refilled it and then scooted into the chair next to mine. Finally, I said, "So have you figured out what to do with them?"

"With what?" he asked.

"Your feelings."

"Oh," he said. "Right."

The next thirty seconds of silence was so painful I thought I'd go fetal right then and there. Imagine my surprise when I suddenly felt Eli's cold hands cupping my face and his coffee-warmed mouth pressing against mine.

Whoa—the plane actually took off while I was writing this and I didn't even notice. Weird, huh? Must take quick bathroom break and then will finish romantic recap.

11/24—A little less ridiculously early in the morning

Couldn't take bathroom break when planned because the plane was about to land in Chicago and I had to switch flights. Was so frantic about finding a place to pee that I almost missed flight number two. But I squeaked in at the last second, sinking into my luxuriously upholstered seat. Oh, and the towels! Hot, lemon-scented towels! Good coffee served in a ceramic mug with real cream! Godiva chocolates available upon request!

Oh, first class—how I've missed thee!

So where was I? Oh, right. The kiss. *The* kiss. A kiss-to-end-all-kisses kind of kiss.

At the end, all I could say was, "Wow."

And all he could say was, "Yeah."

Then Eli took my hands in his and said, "Morgan—I'm so sorry. I don't know why I've been acting like such a jerk. Can you—do you think you might—how about a second chance?"

I resisted the urge to ask, "Isn't this, like, the third chance?" Totally would have broken the mood. Instead, I replied, "Only if you agree to give me one too."

Eli nodded, and my body flooded with hot tingles. Then there was more kissing and a little bit of hands-through-the-hair action, and for a while, we moved to the couch to make out because it was so much more comfortable than the dining room chairs. Whatever problems Eli was having with me before had clearly taken a hike—if the telltale bulge in his pj's was any indication.

Since I knew I wasn't ready to go any further—on a couch? With Trudy asleep in the next room? Only seconds after reconciliation? Uh, no.

I made an excuse to get up and pack. Eli got himself a *huge* glass of water from the kitchen—needing to cool down, I suppose—but then he came into my room and helped me load the suitcase.

Turns out, he's a whiz at this packing thing, too. Showed me how to roll my shirts so that they'd take up less space *and* stay wrinkle-free during the transition. When I looked at him, half incredulously, he offered a cutie-boy grin and said, "We used to go camping a lot. Up in Michigan?

You learn how to fit a lot of stuff into a little bag."

I eyed the suitcase with admiration. "Astounding."

"Listen, about that scene in the cafeteria," he said. "Emily's really sorry too. She overreacted. And she knows it."

"I understand," I told him. "Tell her it's all good."

He left around 3:30 a.m., which gave him about three and a half hours before he'd have to be at school and gave me about an hour before Thaddeus was set to arrive. I took the quickest (coldest) shower ever, humming under my breath the entire time. I even put on a little makeup before shoving my hair under the Fort Wayne Wizards baseball cap Mrs. Whitmarsh bought me right after I'd moved here. Before she had decided that I was the spawn of Satan and needed to quarantine her kids from my evil clutches, that is.

I'd win her over eventually, I decided. And maybe, if I was photographed with the cap on, she'd get the message that I hadn't given up yet.

Holy crap! The pilot just said we'd be landing at LAX in a little under an hour. Time sure does fly when you're young and in love. Ha! Time flies when you're flying. Literally!

Whoo boy. Methinks I am giddy with fatigue. Let me squeeze in a quick nap before it's time to land. . . .

11/24—Much, much later

I've been in L.A. for almost sixteen hours, and I haven't had a single second to myself.

Actually, that's not entirely true. Marissa was about fifteen minutes late picking me up, so by the time she came, I was the only one left in the terminal. I felt small and embarrassed until I realized that Marissa was being followed by an entire crew of photographers. I know I complain about hacks all the time, but that's when I'm in Fort Wayne. Here, it's kind of nice to know that I'm still relevant. Or at the very least, relevant by proxy.

Marissa hugged me—and we squealed our hellos. It was like being the ball in a pinball machine. Lights were flashing all around us. For once, I was glad to have my picture taken. Now the world would have proof that Marissa and I were still totally tight.

After they got their shots, the horde disappeared to wherever it had come from—probably to call photo agencies or favorite, well-paying rag editors.

Even though it was only around 8 a.m., navigating LAX was a nightmare. We headed down to baggage, and Marissa complained that she hadn't had to get her own luggage, like, *ever*, so I told her to go pull the car around and I'd meet her at the exit.

So I wait and I wait and I wait, but my suitcase never comes. Long story short, it's still in Fort Wayne. I try to bribe some baggage dude to FedEx it using Sam's account number, but he says that's against policy. I try to explain to him that I need my luggage *today*, but he says that since I'm coming back Saturday night, he doesn't feel comfortable sending it out at all.

I go out front and look for Marissa's silver Lexus, but it's nowhere to be found. That's because Marissa's traded in her limited edition convertible for an ice blue—I'm sorry, "seaside pearl"—*Toyota Prius*.

"What's up, Ed Begley Junior?" I quipped as I climbed in.

She shot me a cranky look. "Sorry, my dear, but you are way out of date. Everyone's switching to the hybrid cars.

Cameron, Leo—hell, even Will Ferrell drives one."

"And if Will Ferrell drove his Prius off the 110 inter-change, would you follow suit?"

Another look.

"They lost my luggage," I informed her as I buckled up. "So you might as well take off."

"Excellent!" she said, not at all sarcastically.

I was about to ask her what her problem was when I realized why she was so jazzed.

Now we had a reason to go shopping.

As if we'd needed one.

"You know," I mused, "I do have a closet full of clothes at home."

"Except your home isn't your home anymore, remember? Bianca moved into Sam's place since he's got the better pool. Speaking of, you're supposed to call her and check in."

"Jesus, Marissa. I think you talk to the woman more than I do."

"Correction, my little dumpling," she said. "My *assistant* spends more time talking to Bianca's assistant, who, by the way, is gorgeous in that 'I don't have to wear makeup because my skin is naturally luminous' sort of way."

"She won't last long," I scoffed. "My mother can't stand to spend too much time around anyone prettier than she is."

It was still hours before Bianca's standard wakeup time, so I called Sam's office instead. He was in a meeting—when is he not?—and I left a terse but still somewhat amiable message that I had landed safely, had zero luggage, and was going to do some damage to the emergency credit card he'd sent just before the *Oprah* appearance.

My stomach was lurching at this point because between

rehab and my stint in the Fort, I'd forgotten how insane post-rush-hour traffic is on the 405. Marissa kept taking her celeb-endorsed Prius from zero to eighty and back to zero in a screeching halt, all in a matter of minutes, screaming road rage-y things at the surrounding cars.

"Oh, and I almost forgot," Marissa said, after calling a Porsche driver who cut her off an "aging ass rod with a tiny brain and a penis to match." (And this is Marissa without caffeine, mind you, since we had yet to stop for java.) "You have a two o'clock with Lori at John Frieda," she informed me. "Bianca said she thinks your hair color photographs too flat."

"Do you think," I wondered aloud, "that there is a pant color that would make my ass photograph flatter?"

"Nah," she said. "But I hear that laying off the Scooby Snacks helps."

I pinched her arm, hard, and she pinched me right back. Then she pinched my arm again. And again. I told her to quit it and she goes, "Shit, Morgan—you've been toning up, haven't you?" I said not really and then told her about Fabrizio and Bianca's Boot Camp.

Marissa nodded approvingly. "You keep him on the payroll—those arms are about thirty seconds away from pre-buffness." This, I think, is her version of a compliment.

Anyway, Marissa suggested we start on Melrose. At Miss Sixty I found a gorgeous pair of size-eight Suprema jeans and discovered that they were way too big on me. Marissa grabbed the size six version of the same jeans and I wanted to sing loudly when I pulled them on and they were only slightly snug at the waist. At the height of my coke binge-ing, I'd wasted down to a size zero, which Bianca had found enviable (at her lowest weight, she can squeeze into a six). The press, however, stopped praising me when I hit a size two; at this lower weight, they started running pictures of me with captions like, "Somebody buy this girl a sandwich!" Such a fine line between thin and anorexic in this town.

At Fred Segal, I snagged a luscious cranberry-colored Rebecca Taylor cami and a handful of T-shirts by Trunk. Then it was on to my personal mecca—*Marc Jacobs!*—where I scored a charcoal tank dress with a lace yoke and velvet collar (perfect for the Thanksgiving party) and a burgundy-and-charcoal-striped sweater that would look fabulous with my new jeans. I also picked up a handful of tops and some shoes and other utterly gorgeous things I couldn't possibly say no to.

But the big purchase of the day was the dark teal crushed baby doll dress with the satin-sashed empire waist. From the minute I slipped it on, I felt like I had pixie dust running through my veins. I could see myself, hair piled high in some kind of sexy updo, floating into the Winter Wonderdance with Eli by my side, looking smashing in something I'd pick out for him later. I was dreaming of what kind of corsage I'd ask him to get me when Marissa interrupted my reverie to remind me that I needed shoes before my color appointment.

By the time we walked into John Frieda, I'd gotten a pair of Armani black satin ballerina flats and some exquisite Christian Louboutin satin slingbacks the same color as the sash on my Winter Wonderdance dress (hello, kismet!), in addition to the chocolate brown suede wrap boots I'd picked up at Marc Jacobs.

At the salon, Lori, my super-chic stylist, gave me

caramel-colored highlights and chocolate lowlights. We ran into Mandy Moore as we were heading out and decided to grab a late lunch at the Ivy. Mandy gossiped about Adrian Grenier, with whom she'd worked on *Entourage*, this comedy series I'd only read about in *Entertainment Weekly* (Trudy refuses to pay for an HBO upgrade, on account of how much the cable company gouges for it). Marissa watches it religiously, though, and tells me it's "frickin' hilarious."

Then Colin Hanks, who was sitting a few tables over, finished up lunch with his boys, and he stopped by and welcomed me "home." He'd filled out lots since I guested on *Roswell*, and I told him how hot he was looking. He grinned and said I wasn't looking so bad myself, and the whole thing felt so natural that it seemed just like the old days, except for the being-sober part.

It made me think about how even a year ago, I wouldn't have been able to get through my poached salmon without at least two glasses of Vouvray, or a Bellini, or a pitcher of sangria. Why? Why? Even though I'd been nervous about coming back to L.A., and still had that slightly floaty feeling you get after anxiety dissipates, when the waiter asked me what I'd wanted to drink, I didn't hesitate for a single second. Instead, I said, "Unsweetened iced tea, no lemon," without missing a beat of Mandy's account of a trip she and Zach had taken to Machu Picchu.

It was seventy-two degrees and sunny, with a sweet, jasmine-scented breeze dancing in the air. I took in a deep breath.

"You okay?" Marissa asked.

I said, "Do you smell that?"

"What?" Marissa said. "Smog?"

I told her that I meant the jasmine, but she said I must be smelling someone's perfume or something.

Then our drinks arrived, and I discovered how absolutely fantastic the iced tea is at the Ivy. I kept saying it, too—"Oh my God, this is the best iced tea ever. Isn't this the best iced tea you've ever had?"—until Marissa kicked me under the table. Mandy was flashing her worried looks, and I knew what she was thinking.

"I'm not high," I assured her. "In fact, I don't know that I've ever been this sober before. I mean, the whole world seems . . . I don't know. More focused? It's like I had laser surgery on my senses or something."

"Yeah," Marissa said slowly. "Um, don't feel like you have to share every single thought that crosses your mind, okay?"

After lunch, we said goodbye to Mandy and I called Mama B. to see what time she wanted me at the house for dinner. Only, get this: she and Sam had already made dinner plans, and they didn't include me! She said she figured I'd rather be with Marissa—and I guess she was right, but still!—and that I should feel free to spend the night at M.'s place or at Sam's, whatever I was most comfortable with.

Marissa was ecstatic, which made me feel sort of loved, and she called Dotti and gave her a list of errands to run so that we could have the perfect girls' night in. This included getting a house call from Solita, Marissa's favorite mani/pedi tech, and David, who gives great in-home facials. So now my pores are shrunken, my nails gleam cranberry red, and my tummy is still full from all the great sushi Dotti got from Koi.

If I'm not careful, I could really get used to this kind of life.

Again, I mean.

It's almost three in the morning back in Fort Wayne, but I so want to call Eli. However, calling Eli at three in the morning does not seem like the kind of thing that will help me get back into anyone's good graces—including his. Actually, now that I think about it, I'm going to vow right here and now *not* to call Eli until I'm safely back in the Fort. I will, however, pick him up a little something-something on Friday—maybe a new accessory for his lomo cam?

For now, the sleep monster is calling my name. And I must obey.

11/25—a.k.a. Thanksgiving Day

Things I Wish I Could Be Thankful for but Really Am Not:

1. The driver of the town car Bianca sent to pick me up at Marissa's was, like, twelve years old and kept insisting that I was Lindsay Lohan.

2. The room in Sam's house designated as "mine" is painted mud brown because Bianca heard from Sarah Jessica Parker's decorator that it's the new "in" color.

3. In moving my belongings from our old house, my mother decided to weed out all of the things in my closet that she thought were unflattering to me and donated them to Goodwill.

4. This includes about eight seasons' worth of Marc Jacobs, including a couple of couture pieces that Marc had gifted to me himself.

5. She also decided to donate my library of scripts to some museum of film and television, but when I Googled the name of it, I couldn't find such a museum.

6. A quick search on eBay, however, turned up several of the titles, which means my mother helped some degenerate make his beer money off auctioning off *my* irreplaceable library.

7. I put in several bids on my script from *Girls on Top* but lost out to baybeegrl7 by exactly fifty-three cents during an ill-timed pee break.

8. Bianca thinks the dress I bought for the Travoltas' Thanksgiving party is too low-key and is insisting I instead wear this hideous slip dress she bought me. It's in the most obnoxious shade of pumpkin, and the satin fabric highlights the small bump of my belly.

9. When I refused to don said dress, she asked me if I'd put on weight.

10. When I told her no, that I had in fact lost several pounds (thanks to Fabrizio), she told me it must be the pink T-shirt I was wearing that made me look so piggish.

Yeah, it's really great to be "home."

11/25—*Later*

This place is depressing. Even more depressing is how much my mother's vanity has grown now that she's married to *the* Sam Rosenbaum. She feels like she has a "station" to fill. At least, that's what she told me when I asked why she'd hired hair and makeup people to come to the house pre-party.

"You're turning into Sharon Osbourne," I whined. "Next thing I know, you'll be wanting to pimp me out to reality TV."

Her mouth opened slightly, then closed into a long, thin line.

I said, "Please tell me you're not even *thinking* about something that asinine. You know what those shows do to people, Mother."

But all Bianca said was, "Don't forget to wear hose with your dress."

There is absolutely no way I'm wearing that orange rag she bought. Especially not with the pistachio-colored wrap that she thinks looks "darling" with it. Hello, is the Travoltas' house on *Sesame Street*?

Am seriously wanting to call E. but must remain strong, strong, strong until Saturday night.

Time for hair and makeup!

11/25—*Much later*

I'm hiding out in a spare bedroom on the second floor of the house owned by John Travolta and Kelly Preston, writing this on the pretty cream-and-gold stationery they left in a drawer of the antique mahogany rolltop desk, and I can't stop shaking.

Okay. Deep breaths.

Here's what happened:

The limo arrived around six. Bianca and I got in and drove to Sam's office, since he'd spent the entire day working. This was actually the first time I'd seen him since I arrived in California, and it was weird because even though he gave me a hug, it felt weak and he refused to look me in the eye. I felt like he and Bianca were cooking something up that I was definitely *not* going to like, but I was too nervous about this party thing to care.

Oh, and by the way—I won the dress fight. Except I did

end up using the pistachio-colored wrap, as it looked quite lovely against the charcoal.

Anyway.

So we arrive at this party, and there are cameras everywhere. I mean, *everywhere*. And everybody with a camera has lights, so the place is flooded to the point that you could barely see a foot ahead of you. I guess I'd known there'd be press here, but God, how embarrassing to be photographed with my *parents*. Parent and stepparent? Parent and manager-slash-stepparent? Whatever. Very lame.

I smiled and posed for about half an hour before Marissa arrived (thank God!), and she helped me get out of Bianca's clutches. Everyone was downing glasses of champagne and my throat started itching, so Marissa loaded up a plate of pumpkin canapés and mini squash quiches and steered me toward the back patio.

There was a guy in a black suit who had followed us out there. He kept touching his ear, like there was a transmitter in there or something, and mumbling in a low voice. Actually, he kind of looked like a Secret Service agent.

"Is the president here?" I asked Marissa. "I thought these guys were Democrats."

Marissa shook her head. "No, that's one of those Scientology guys. See the pin on his lapel?"

"Dude," I groaned. "Fully disturbing."

"Just ignore him," she instructed. She pulled a cigarette out of a dark blue pack. "Want one?" she said. "They're French."

I tried smoking several years back, but it never "took." Even with pot—I always inhaled better with a bong than a joint or a pipe. Don't ask me why. For some reason, though,

Marissa's cig looked tempting. Maybe because everything felt so *raw*.

It was like . . . like the flip side of what I'd been feeling at the Ivy yesterday. I might be able to smell jasmine in the air, but I could also smell the sweet tang of liquor everywhere I turned.

And then it happened. At first, I thought I was seeing things. Because that's happened before, you know. I'd be at a restaurant or, in the old days, some club, and I'd think I'd see him. When really, it was always some nameless brown-haired guy who, on closer inspection, looked nothing like the bastard.

But there he was.

Harlan Darly.

The bastard himself.

He was just standing there, typically underdressed in designer jeans and a blazer, swirling the ice at the bottom of his drink.

I dug my fingernails into the flesh of Marissa's forearm. "Please tell me that isn't who I think it is," I said.

She asked me who I was talking about, and I said his name. It came out barely above a whisper.

"Yeah, that's him," she said. "What's the deal with you two, anyway? Dotti said he's been telling anyone who'd listen that you're, like, the love of his life. I always thought you hated the dude, though you still haven't told me *why*."

The only people I *had* told had no connection to this portion of my life. Plus, how could I explain to Marissa now, when I'd kept it a secret for so long? And what if she judged me—told me it was my fault for getting so wasted, told me that if I hadn't been so screwed up on drugs and alcohol, Harlan Darly wouldn't have been able to do what he did?

Marissa was staring at me expectantly, waiting for me to spill whatever I was holding up tight inside me. Finally, I said, "I lost my virginity to him."

"Oh." Marissa waved her hand as if to say, "No biggie." Then she grinned wickedly. "Was it really bad? The sex, I mean."

"You could say that."

"I always had a feeling about him," she said knowingly. "You can just tell he's got a cocktail weenie instead of a ball-park frank. I mean, he's so *short*. Am I right?"

My eyes filled up with tears, and I turned to speak into Marissa's ear. "He raped me," I said softly. "Three years ago, he raped me."

When I pulled away, I could see that Marissa's mouth had formed a tight O. Then her eyes narrowed. "I'll kill the son of a bitch."

"No!" I said, a little too loudly. "No, don't. Just . . . just forget I said anything."

She looked at me like I'd suddenly morphed into a pre–TrimSpa Anna Nicole Smith. "Morgan," she breathed. "Why didn't you ever tell me?"

"I was embarrassed," I said. "I still am."

"Because somebody raped you?" she asked incredulously. I shook my head and shushed her, digging my nails in deeper.

"Just . . . shut up about it," I pleaded.

"No," Marissa said, with force. "This is *not* the Morgan Carter I've grown up with. You don't take shit from any-body. What's so special about Harlan dick-faced Darly that makes you want to hide in the bushes? Jesus, Morgan. *Jesus.*"

"I was drunk," I said flatly. "And high. And I can't remember if I ever said no."

"Do you remember saying yes?" she asked. "No, don't answer that. I don't even care! You were what? Fourteen? I don't care if you *begged* him to ball you—it was wrong. Do you hear me? *Wrong*."

"Please, just let it go," I said. "I have."

She snorted. "Right, you've moved so far past it that seeing the asshole from across the room is enough to make you turn eight shades of green." Marissa finished her cigarette, pinched off the ash, stomped it, and threw the butt in Harlan Darly's direction. "You know what you've got to do."

I shook my head.

"You've got to face him. Tonight. Drag him to some back bedroom and ram your knee into his groin. He can't do much damage to anyone else if he's got a smashed cocktail weenie for a weapon."

I thought about it for like a second, then shook my head again. "No," I said, as firmly as I could. "I have to pee."

And then I ran away from her as fast as my three-inch heels would let me. Too bad I wasn't paying closer attention, because the next thing I knew, I'd run right into *him*.

"Where's the fire, darlin'?" he joked in his slow southern drawl.

Recognition flashed across his face.

"Hey, you," he said. "I was hoping I'd see you here."

I was so shocked to be standing face-to-face with him. This monster who'd haunted my nightmares for the past three years. Harlan grinned at me, his dimples diving deep into his cheeks.

"Did you catch me on *Leno*?" he asked, placing his non-drink-holding hand on my elbow in this possessive kind of way. "Everybody's talking about it."

I couldn't speak. It was like someone had stolen my voice straight from my throat.

Harlan leaned in toward me and said, "You look really hot tonight." His breath smelled like whiskey.

I stepped backward, and Harlan stumbled slightly.

"Hey," he said. "Where you going, beautiful?"

Please, I prayed silently. *Just let me go.*

Harlan downed the contents of his glass, wiped a little extra whiskey from the side of his mouth, and said, "We better walk the gauntlet before the hacks use up all their film. And nothing too posed, okay, sweetheart? My publicist wants candids."

Harlan started steering me toward the row of photographers by the front of the house. What had he been smoking? There was no way I was going to further this stupid stunt. Bad enough that Bianca cooked it up—at least she didn't know about Harlan's and my history. But him? Expecting me to play along? Was he really that pathological?

Flashbulbs were already popping when I finally regained some semblance of composure. I turned to sprint down the hall. Harlan grabbed my hand for a second, but I shook it off quickly. Deep in the recesses of the first floor, I found an unlocked bathroom and dove inside.

He followed me. The son of a bitch actually followed me.

"Slow down, baby girl," he said, his voice slightly slurred. "You and me got all night."

Harlan leaned forward like he was going to kiss me, but before his lips could touch mine, I ducked. Then I ran into the frosted-glass–paned shower stall and locked myself in it.

Harlan, too drunk to realize I was trying to ditch him, fumbled with the latch on the door. "Uh, Morgan?" he said. "I'm totally into the shower thing, but babe? You've gotta open up."

Feeling somewhat safer behind the glass, I was able to muster up a hoarse, "Go away."

"What was that?" Harlan asked. "You need a drink or something?"

"Go away!" I repeated in a slightly louder tone.

"Huh?"

"GO. A. WAY." I pounded my fists against the glass, rattling the panes. "Go away! Go away! Go *away!*"

"Man," Harlan said, slow and slurred. "You were way more fun when you were loaded."

I could not believe this was happening. And I certainly couldn't believe what he'd just said.

The bathroom door slammed shut, and when I was certain I was alone, I stepped out of the shower stall and collapsed onto the toilet seat, shaking. Three years of dreading this moment—three years of planning what I'd say if this moment ever happened—and I hid in a shower stall? Screaming "go away" like a psycho on a third-grade reading level?

All I could think was, *I need a drink. I need a drink.*

I deserve a drink.

So I made a beeline for the bar.

"Glenlivet, neat," I said, not caring who saw or heard. Well, I must've cared a little, because I noticed a newly thinned-out Kirstie Alley standing next to me, with a look of surprise and concern splayed on her face. "Fuck it," I said, more to me than her, and when the bartender pushed the crystal tumbler my way, I lifted it straight to my mouth.

The second the amber liquid burned the back of my throat, my body rejected it. I turned just in time to puke my guts up on Kirstie's pretty gold pumps.

Yeah. That actually happened. I mumbled some kind of apology, and the tumbler crashed to the floor. Which means I probably spilled the rest of my whiskey over top of the puke, thereby ensuring that Kirstie Alley will permanently remove me from her Christmas card list (and rightly so).

A bunch of people swarmed around me, asking me if I was okay, and I assured them I was, even though I wasn't.

"Must've been the shrimp," I said repeatedly.

Then, feeling like I couldn't bear to face anyone—not even Marissa—I ran off to this second-floor guest room and locked the door. I've been hiding out here ever since.

It's going on eleven now, and I'm sure Bianca is freaking out that I'm nowhere to be seen. Marissa too, for that matter. My cell has rung half a dozen times, but I refuse to answer it until I'm good and ready (i.e., until I can stop shaking).

11/25—Much, much later

I wonder, does it ruin your sobriety if liquor fills your mouth but you never actually swallow? Because I'm supposed to be getting my one-year chip soon, and it would really suck if I had to start counting over from day one.

11/25—Much, much, much later

I fell asleep in the guest room, and some maid had to come find me. Bianca is beyond livid. It didn't help that when she found me, I was groggy and still smelling slightly of whiskey.

"I heard you gave Kirstie Alley an early Christmas

present," she said nastily, taking me by the arm—*hard*. "Say goodbye to freedom, Morgan, because tomorrow your ass is going back to rehab."

She refused to listen to me the whole limo ride home, taking the more passive-aggressive stance of asking Sam to tell me she couldn't stand looking at me, let alone hearing the sound of my voice. I begged her to set aside her anger for just a minute so I could explain, but Bianca was having none of it. Eventually, Sam cut in and said, "We'll talk in the morning, honey. We all just need a good night's sleep."

But the minute we hit the house, Bianca stormed off to the kitchen and returned with a handheld machine that had a hose coming off one end. She pushed some buttons and handed the contraption to me. "Blow," she commanded.

"What is that thing?"

She didn't answer, just repeated her instructions. "Blow."

So I did, and she read the meter, and by this point, I realized it was a home Breathalyzer kit. Her eyes narrowed and she reset the machine, telling me to blow again. I did, and since I knew I hadn't been drinking, I knew the meter must've come up blank.

"See?" I said. "Now do you believe me?"

Sam took the machine gently from Bianca's hands. "Morgan, honey," he said. "Please, just go to bed. Please. We'll talk in the morning."

It's now almost 6 a.m. and I still can't sleep, even though I'm exhausted from the inside out. Marissa's left four more messages on my cell, each one sounding more and more worried. I'm a shit for not calling her back, but I'm just not ready to deal. And I'm definitely *not* going back to rehab, no matter what Bianca says. I might have almost screwed up, but in the end I didn't.

Finally, something to be thankful for.

11/26

I slept through half the day and would probably still be sleeping if Marissa hadn't practically torn down the bedroom door.

"Why didn't you call me back?" she yelled, shaking me. "Morgan Maria Carter, I have been worried *sick* about you. Literally, I've been throwing up. What happened last night? Where did you go? Why didn't you answer your phone?"

"I'm sorry," I mumbled, still half asleep. She yelled at me some more until I'd woken up enough to know I needed to pee. So I went to the bathroom, and when I came back, I told her everything, right down to the Glenlivet mouthwash and my unfortunate incident with Kirstie Alley's shoes.

"Holy shit!" she said. "I kinda heard about the puking thing. I mean, it happened at the bar, so people were talking. And then when Bianca couldn't find you . . . but don't worry, I've already talked to her. I told her that Harlan Darly was trying to pressure you into getting high and that you got away but felt queasy, and that's why you puked on Kirstie's shoes. Then when she asked me why you smelled like whiskey, I said it was actually Kirstie's drink, and she was so startled by your little upchuck incident that *she* spilled the drink on you."

"Wow," I said. "You're good."

"Yeah, well, I'm not letting anyone send you back to rehab. Especially since I knew you didn't take that drink. It was just like Chicago, right? You wanted to, but you would never throw away your sobriety like that. Right?"

"Actually," I said, letting out a long, deep breath, "if I hadn't puked, I would've swallowed. So please—don't make me out to be all noble."

She thought about this for a second, then said, "No. See, you wouldn't have puked if you really wanted that drink. Your reflex was to obliterate the bad stuff, just like always. But your brain knew better. It wouldn't let you screw it all up. As far as I'm concerned, you're still due for that one-year chip. And don't let anyone tell you otherwise."

Marissa put her arms around me, and I cried a little onto her bare shoulder. She rubbed my back and kept saying things like, "It's okay, Morgan. It's going to be okay. *You're* going to be okay."

She left about an hour ago, and I took a long, hot shower. But I'm still too chicken to face Bianca. I'm even more chicken to face Sam.

I thought that by coming here I could get away for my problems for a little while. But the problems here are even *worse*.

I should've just stayed in Fort Wayne.

11/26—Later

Sam and I just had the strangest heart-to-heart. He came up to my room around 2 p.m. and asked me to come to the kitchen. There, set on the island, was a little bamboo tray with coffee and a plateful of matzo brei—the one dish Sam knows how to make. He used to bring me some every time I lost out on a big part, much to Bianca's dismay (she hates that it's cooked in chicken fat). In fact, Bianca hates most Jewish soul food for this very reason—too much fat, too many carbs—so I imagine it's been a while since Sam's been able to whip up a batch of fried matzo.

I asked him where Bianca was, and he said she'd gone to the spa with one of her infamous headaches. Apparently, hot stone massages and kelp wraps relieve her "migraines."

I said, "I guess it's good that I'm flying home tomorrow night, huh?" and he goes, "Why would you say that?"

"Well," I said, "all I seem to do is cause Bianca pain—real or imagined."

He shook his head. "Your mother loves you, kitten. She's just worried about you."

"If she's so worried about me, then why doesn't she ever call me?" I shot back.

Sam sighed. "You probably won't understand this, but she thinks you don't need her anymore."

"Need?" I said. "That's what this is about?"

He said, "Most parents don't have to deal with this kind of separation until their kids go off to college."

"Most parents don't put their children to work before their first birthday, either," I replied.

Sam pushed the plate of matzo closer to me. "Eat," he said.

When I'd downed a fair amount, I said, "Hey, Sam—why don't *you* ever call me? Do you think I stopped needing you too?"

"No, no," he said. "It's not that."

"Then what?"

"I've been your manager since you were what—an infant? But now I'm your stepdad, too. I don't know where

164

to draw the line between those roles, you know? Plus, you're trying to have this normal adolescent experience. You don't need your agent checking up on you every five minutes."

"True," I said. "But I wouldn't mind hearing my stepdad's voice once in a while."

He smiled, the crinkly wrinkles around his eyes growing deeper. "Can you . . . can you think of me in that way?"

I put the fork down on my plate and said, "Sam, you've been the only dad I've ever known. All the sperm donor ever does is try to wheedle money out of me and Mama B. But you—you've been my everything. You know that."

"Then why," he asked, "were you so upset about me marrying your mom?"

I told him that for one thing, it was bad form to marry a person's mother without inviting the daughter to the ceremony. Or to tie the knot before even informing said daughter that a courtship had been going on.

"But mostly, I was worried that she was . . . you know. Using you. For status. Wealth. All the things I could no longer provide."

He let out a deep breath. "Morgan. Honey, no. I've watched your mother tear her way through her fair share of eligible bachelors, and maybe her intentions weren't always . . . pure. But your mother does love me, Morgan. I am certain of that."

"And what about you?" I asked. "Do you love her too?"

"Yeah. Yeah, I do."

"But *why*?" I practically whined. "She's so—"

"Unique," he finished for me. "Just like you are."

"I was going to say 'manipulative.'"

Sam didn't answer. Instead, he grabbed a bottle of Perrier from the stainless steel fridge and poured us each a glass.

"Lime?" he asked.

"You have to stop this nonsense with Harlan Darly," I blurted.

Sam did a double take.

"Please," I said. "I know you think you need him as a client, but there are other actors who are, like, way better and way younger and have way more potential."

"What do you have against Harlan Darly?" he asked.

Now it was my turn to not answer because I didn't know what to say. I'd already disappointed Sam so many times—how could I add this to the list? Plus, it would change the way he'd look at me forever. It was bad enough in the hospital, right after I'd OD'd. The mixture of shock and sadness and anger and . . . guilt. I knew he felt guilty for not putting a stop to things sooner, even though none of it was his fault.

I couldn't tell him about what happened between me and Harlan Darly. I just couldn't.

"Does this have something to do with that Eli kid?" Sam asked.

"Sort of," I said. "Yeah, that's it. Eli. That's why you need to stop the Harlan story."

Sam shook his head. "What does he expect? An average little nothing dating an international movie star? Of course he's going to be a target."

"Stop," I said sharply. "Eli isn't an 'average little nothing.' He's someone I care about. A lot. He's . . . he's one of my best friends, Sam, and nothing about your Witless Protection Program would've worked without him and Emily."

He sighed. "We didn't send you there so you could go

steady with some common teenager. You're supposed to be focusing on your studies and your sobriety."

"Oh, really?" I said. "Is that why Bianca has every second of my day scheduled with the trainer, the facialist, the voice coach, the dance teacher? She forgot to pencil in time for homework, you know. Not to mention my weekly meetings. So don't act like Eli is some big distraction, okay? He's not the problem. *She* is."

"Let me put it another way," Sam said slowly. "Now is not the time to bait your mother. She's thirty seconds away from sending you back to rehab."

"Why?" I shrilled. "I'm almost one year sober!"

"She doesn't like you being out there. In Fort Wayne. She wants you here, with us."

A bitter laugh escaped my mouth. "She has a funny way of showing it."

Sam uncapped the Perrier again, but instead of pouring some into his glass, he drank straight from the bottle.

"Shhh," he said, grinning. "Your mom hates when I do that."

I pushed myself away from the table. "So I guess that's it, then."

Sam leaned over and kissed my forehead. "Don't worry," he said. "You're not going to back to rehab. And you'll finish the school year in Fort Wayne, like we agreed. After that, well, we'll talk. But while you're here . . . think you can make nice with your mother? If not for her, then for me?"

"Sure," I said. "Whatever."

He told me that he'd made reservations for all of us at Dolce's for 8 p.m. and that if I really wanted to smooth things over with my mom, I'd wear that stupid pumpkin-colored dress.

The thing that burns me the most? She always wins. Bianca, I mean. Because I'm going to have to do it.

I'm actually going to have to wear that fugly orange dress.

11/26—Much, much later

Dinner = okay. Bennifer II was there, and her stomach looked so flat you could hardly believe they'd just had Baby Bennifer. Bianca wanted me to go up to them since I know Ben, but they looked like they were having a romantic meal and I didn't want to interrupt. They got their check long before we got ours, and surprisingly enough, Ben made a point to come by our table to say hello.

He swooped down and gave me a big bear hug and said how nice it was to see me, and in my ear, he whispered, "You're doing good, girlie. Keep it up." I introduced him to Bianca and Sam, both of whom he'd met before, and he introduced us to Jennifer, as if we didn't know who she was. We made small talk for a few, and just before they left, Ben said that he and Matt were polishing a new screenplay and there might be a part in it for me, so I should give him a ring. Bianca's eyes flashed at Sam, like she was saying, "Get her this part!" and then Ben gave me a kiss on the cheek and Jennifer said, "Nice to meet you all," and with big smiles, they were gone.

The weirdest thing? It was probably the most "normal" moment I'd had since I'd flown back to Los Angeles. Normal, yet completely foreign and odd, if we're talking in Fort Wayne terms.

I guess that's the problem. I don't know whose terms to use anymore—mine or Claudia's.

Maybe I'm still in shock over last night's incident with Harlan Darly—I don't know. What I do know is that when Ben told me about the potential role, I didn't get that rush of excitement I used to when there was a part I wanted to go after. Instead, I felt a cold dread creep over me.

Wonder what that means . . .

When we got back, Bianca and I had a quick conversation about what happened at the Travoltas', and she said that Marissa had explained most of it and that there'd be no further talk of rehab unless I felt I needed to go back. I told her that I didn't and that she had nothing to worry about, but then remembering what Sam said earlier, I added, "Although it would be nice if you would come out to Fort Wayne again. For a real visit this time. I'd like to show you around, introduce you to some of my friends. And I know that Trudy would like to spend some time with you too."

She smiled then, a genuine sort of smile, and impulsively gave me a hug. It felt good to be hugged by her, and for once, I was glad I'd put forth the extra effort.

Then she said, "Morgan, dear—promise me you'll see that trainer I got you at least three times a week. You're beginning to feel a little too soft in the middle."

Sigh. So much for maternal instincts.

11/27

Sam said goodbye this morning. He had to fly out to Vegas because one of his other clients (who shall remain name-less) went on a Vicodin-and-booze binge and ended up destroying the penthouse suite at the Palms. Bianca had scheduled us to have a mother-daughter brunch with Goldie and Kate, but then Kate's kid got sick, so I told Bianca to go on without me.

As soon as she left, I called the airline and changed my ticket to a much-earlier flight. Then I called Marissa and asked her if she could take me to the airport so I'd have a chance to say goodbye.

"No," she said.

This surprised me, especially since she'd been encouraging me to stay in Fort Wayne. I told her that it was okay and that I'd call a car service. Then she said, "No, I don't want you to go! You just got here!"

"I know," I said. "It's just . . . well . . . L.A. doesn't feel like home anymore." My voice came out small and quiet. "I don't think I really have a home."

"I'm your home," she said. "I'm your family."

I knew she meant it, too. We'd been through so much together. And I did miss her when I was in Indiana—I missed her terribly. But I couldn't see how staying in Los Angeles was going to help me move forward, and I'm really tired of spending all of my time looking back.

I told her that I was sorry and that she was welcome to visit anytime. And I told her I'd be back in a month for Christmas, when I'd have more time off from school. Though even as I said it, I was thinking I wouldn't want to spend my whole vacation in California since it might be fun to have a white Christmas in Fort Wayne—going ice skating with Eli and Emily, making a snowman with Trudy in the front yard, hanging out with the cast from *Oklahoma!* with whom I'd invariably be bonded by that time.

All she said was, "You suck."

Then, after a pause, she told me to pack and that she'd be at the house by four.

Since I was alone except for the housekeeper, the gardener, and the cook, I spent the next hour rifling through what was left of my wardrobe, filching just enough pieces to supplement what I had back home but not enough so that Bianca would know I was exporting designer clothes to Fort Wayne. Then I went into her private bathroom and stocked up on unopened MAC lipsticks and other assorted grooming products Bianca would never miss.

She called me from her late lunch with Goldie and told me they were heading over to Tiffany to do a little Christmas shopping and would I like to join them? I said no thanks and that I'd see her at dinner. I purposely neglected to tell her I'd be gone before she got back, afraid she'd try to talk me into staying longer.

Now I'm just waiting for Marissa's Prius to pull up in the driveway. I can't wait to get on that plane. Everything on my body is itching.

It's like I've become allergic to L.A.

11/27—Later

I have never been so mortified in my life.

I knew I should've called Trudy, told her I was taking an earlier flight. Instead, I thought I'd surprise her.

Boy, did I ever.

It was like watching *Being Bobby Brown* on Bravo—you know you should look away, but you can't because it's mesmerizing in its awfulness. The images that are seared into my brain—Trudy and Dave, on the couch, *naked*—

When I realized what I'd walked into and they realized they weren't alone, even big manly Dave screamed like a little girl.

I feel like throwing up.

11/27—Much later

Dave left not long after I'd interrupted his and Trudy's tryst. I can't blame him. After what I've seen, I don't think I'll ever be able to look him in the eye again.

Trudy came into my room, wrapped in a terry-cloth robe, and I tried very hard to pretend that I didn't know what lurked underneath. I stared at my fingernails as I apologized, as sincerely and profusely as I could, but Trudy just laughed.

"It's okay, Morgan," she said. "I mean, I'm sorry you . . . you know. Saw that. But Dave and I are consenting adults, and we're in love, so I can't be ashamed that we were making love."

Okay, someday I'm going to write a parenting handbook, and in it I'm going to have an entire chapter about why adults shouldn't use any sentence with the words "making love" unless they're referring to a mid-seventies classic rock tune by Bad Company. Because seriously? It makes me want to puke.

"We don't need to have this conversation," I said. "Really. I don't care what you and Dave do. And I'm very happy that the two of you are in love. That's . . . all I need to know."

"No, no," she insisted. "We should talk about this. How are you feeling?"

"Besides completely mortified?" I said.

Trudy said, "Forget about embarrassment. I want to know how you feel about me and Dave. You and I don't spend as much time together as we used to. In a way, that's good—it means you're making friends and building a life for yourself here. But I have to admit, I miss hanging out with you. Taking crazy exercise classes at the Y, watching old episodes of *Dawson's Creek* on DVD, getting impromptu mani/pedis from Asian women who make fun of us in their native tongue."

She reached up and smoothed a chunk of hair behind my ear. "I'm thirty-nine years old, Morgan. I might never have a child of my own. While I'm sure you don't think of me as your mother—"

"Considering who my mother is, that's probably a good thing."

Trudy smiled. "You're a good kid, Morgan Carter. And it's nice to see you acting like one for a change. Wait—I mean *being* one for a change. I feel like I'm a part of that. Watching you grow . . ."

"Uh, thanks," I said. "I think."

"What I'm trying to say," she continued, "is that it's not about me helping your mom out or giving you a place to hide. You're like—no, you *are*—my family. I love you very much."

A year ago, I would've considered it a Lifetime Television for Women kind of moment—sappy and manipulative, the kind of thing designed to wrestle a few crocodile tears from your eyes. But this wasn't a year ago, and I felt a few (real) tears fall.

"I love you too," I said. "I wish—I wish I'd spent Thanksgiving with you instead of at John Travolta's house, ralphing all over Kirstie Alley's feet."

Of course, this wasn't the kind of comment that could go without explanation, so I quickly filled her in on the details of my trip—including running into Harlan Darly but leaving out the part about changing my flight without telling Bianca. I figured she'd find that out soon enough.

"You poor thing," she said. "Did you talk to Sam about Darly?"

I said, "I tried, but he wasn't listening. He thought the only reason I wanted him to call it off was because of Eli. I couldn't bring myself to tell him the truth.

"Plus," I continued, "there's this other thing I haven't told you about. Something Sam said about his business. How it, uh, wasn't what it used to be. Before I OD'd, I'm guessing, but he wouldn't say. He only told me that he needed to sign some new high-profile clients."

"Like Harlan Darly," she said. "Jesus, Morgan. He sold you out!"

"It's not like that," I said. "Remember, he doesn't know what happened. And I have no intention of telling him either."

Before we could get any deeper into the subject, I asked her how her Thanksgiving was. She told me all about meeting Dave's family and how their relationship was now on a "deeper" level.

"I know," I said. "I walked in on the depth, remember?"

Trudy buried her face in her hands and groaned. "How much did you see?"

"Enough to make me feel slightly ill," I confessed. "But that's because I sort of do think of you like a mom. And who really wants to watch their mom doing *that*?"

This made her laugh, which made me laugh. Then we hugged, long and hard.

When I got into bed, I couldn't sleep. Probably because I was still on California time. But also, I kept thinking about the way Trudy talked to me, and the way she looked at me, and how there's a warmth about everything she does that I never get to see in Bianca.

With her, it's about showing me off—like I'm an extension of who she is and not my own person. Whereas Trudy's all about me having independence (within reason)—letting me figure out who I am instead of telling me who I am.

11/28

Crap! It's almost 9 p.m. and I *just* woke up. Not a total surprise since I didn't end up falling asleep until, like, seven in the morning. But I've got homework to do, and I still haven't showered, and I'm starving, and all I really want to do is call Eli, but I'm a little ticked off that he hasn't even tried to call me.

Shit, shit, double shit.

11/28—*Later*

I guess things *are* getting back to normal. Emily called just as I was about to get in the shower—around ten or so—and she filled me in on the Caspar situation. (They're still together, but she told him she doesn't know when she'll be ready to sleep with him again. Surprisingly, he is okay with this.) Then she started asking me about my trip, but I was itching for that shower and I still hadn't eaten, so I told her we'd talk after school tomorrow.

I took a long, hot shower, and just as I was drying off,

my cell started ringing again. This time it was Eli, calling to wish me "sweet dreams."

"Wow," I said. "I haven't heard those words in a while."

"I missed saying them," he told me. "Does that sound cheesy?"

"Sort of," I said. "But cheesy in a good way, like Kraft Macaroni and Cheese cheesy."

"You're weird," he said, chuckling. "Pick you up for school?"

"Yes, please," I said. "And bring—"

"Coffee," he finished for me. "I know the drill."

And now it's almost midnight, and I have no idea when I'm going to get sleepy, seeing as I didn't even get up until nine. I've tried warm milk and two kinds of herbal tea, but all that did was make me need to pee every five minutes.

I miss the days of Xanax. Oh, yes I do, yes I do.

11/29

This morning was so picture-perfect, what with Eli bringing me a steaming hot grande Sumatra and delivering it with several kisses that were even hotter, that I totally forgot that Ms. Bowman would be posting the cast list for *Oklahoma!* today. Had I remembered, I might have dressed a little differently. More of the old Claudia wardrobe, less of the Morgan stuff I'd filched from California. Instead, I'd worn a flouncy Betsey Johnson skirt, a petal pink satin camisole with lace trim, and a vintage sharkskin blazer with a white cabbage rose pin on its lapel.

If I'd been hanging out with Mischa Barton, I'd have been getting my picture taken for the pages of *People* magazine. Or *InStyle*. Or something. Instead, I was getting weird looks from everyone, including Principal Barke, who passed me with his perpetual frown tattooed on his face.

And then I saw her. Debbie Ackerman. She was sauntering down the hallway, and when she saw me, a wicked grin appeared on her red-lipsticked mouth.

"Well, if it isn't Little Miss Hollywood," she said, sounding like a typical cast member of *The O.C.* "Really sorry you didn't get the lead, but it looks like Ms. Bowman had you typecast from the start. See you at rehearsal on Wednesday!"

I made a beeline for Ms. Bowman's classroom, trying to look as cool and collected as possible. Delia was waiting for me next to the cast list. She looked like someone who'd inhaled too much helium and was about to pass out from it.

Before I could even read the sheet, Delia exploded. "I'm your understudy!" she squealed. "Me! The understudy to Morgan Carter! Isn't that the best?"

"Congrats," I said weakly. "What part are we playing?"

"Ado Annie! I mean, I know it's not Laurey, but guess who's playing Ali Hakim? That hottie *Luke Paxton*! We *both* get to kiss him!"

Before I could fully process what she was saying, Delia babbled on, "Debbie got Laurey, which I know sucks, but Colin McAfee is Curly and ew, who wants to kiss him? At least you get to mack on Luke. Oh, and Riley got the part of Will, so you've got *two* hot guys you get to smooch instead of a dorky-looking dude whose heterosexuality is definitely in question."

"Delia!" I said, a bit too sharply.

"Oh, I'm sorry," she said, taking a step backward.

I felt bad. "Just . . . let me read the list for myself."

If I had to rank my reaction to what I saw, it would look something like this:

- Debbie getting the role of Laurey, signifying that phase one of OSD was a total failure (-50 pts.);
- Me being cast as Annie, the slutterific comic relief (-50 pts.);
- Me not having to stage-kiss Colin McAfee, who uses Island Breeze lip balm and therefore always looks overly moist (+10 pts.);

- Me getting to share lots of scenes with Riley (+25 pts.);
- LaTanya being bumped up from stage manager to student director (+25 pts.);
- Emily taking LaTanya's place as stage manager (!!!) (+30 pts.).
  TOTAL: –10 pts.

Not bad, considering.

I promised Delia that we could gossip all about the play at lunch but that I needed to go use the ladies' room before first bell. I didn't have to, really, but I couldn't stand listening to her be so pep squad about the whole thing. Forget me having to eat major crow from Debbie Ackerman. That's bad enough. But how could I have not gotten the lead? *I've been nominated for an Academy Award.*

I think I'll see if I can convince Thaddeus to take me home after lunch. Because first of all, I feel like a walking corpse, and second of all . . . I just can't bear to be here right now.

Funny. I really don't want to be anywhere right now.

11/29—Later

Got to talk to Em for like five minutes before English.

I said, "I didn't know you were doing the play!" and she said, "It was supposed to be a surprise!"

Then she gave me an even bigger surprise.

"I was thinking about calling Caspar," she said. "It's about time we visited the arcade."

"No!" I said.

"Yeah," she said. "I think . . . yeah."

This was huge. Maybe even more huge than her and

179

Caspar doing it. As far as I know, I'm the only person in Emily's life who knows about her secret obsession with Dance Dance Revolution. And even then, she's only let me go with her a couple of times. Around the arcade, she's known as "Shorty," and she's even won competitions. The girl is absolutely fierce . . . but also extremely self-conscious about the whole thing. So, for her to be inviting Caspar to go with her . . . well, let's just say that it made me think our Emily was really, really in love.

Still, I am making Thaddeus take me home early.

11/29—Much later

I could kill Delia Lambert.

I mean, her heart was in the right place. She felt bad about phase one of Operation Screw Debbie failing so miserably. So she'd mobilized her phase two troops to take action today—without consulting me first. Which meant that at least one part of phase two did *not* go off as planned because instead of having an airtight alibi, I'd cut all my afternoon classes and spent the rest of the day in bed.

Which no one could prove.

Which meant that when Debbie implicated me in the vandalism, I would have absolutely no defense. Just motive—and opportunity

Also, I didn't get the satisfaction of *seeing* the carnage. Which would have been totally sweet.

The only thing keeping me from actually killing Delia Lambert—besides the illegality of it—is her inspired addition to the original "redecorating" plan.

"I got this pig head antennae ball at the gas station," she

told me gleefully. "Then I superglued it onto Debbie's car."

She told me how proud I'd have been if I'd seen it all. The cheer squad had absolutely *covered* Debbie's car in Silly String. Delia doubted Debbie was even able to get the door open without ripping the mounds and mounds of string off first.

Hee!

Evil? Yes, but also totally re-energizing!

When we got off the phone, I called Riley.

"Heard about what you did to Ackerman's car," he said.

I told him it wasn't me.

"Doesn't matter if you were the executioner," he said. "You ordered the hit."

"So, are you still going to help me with phase three?" I asked.

"You sure you want to go through with it?" Riley asked. "I mean, it's really a terribly cruel thing you're asking me to do."

I said, "Riley, she's the one who outed *me*. She sold me out to the highest bidder. If it wasn't for her, I might still be Claudia Miller, quietly having a normal high school existence."

"You had me at 'outed,'" he said. "I'll start tomorrow."

I can't wait to watch her squirm.

11/30

I found out because someone had taped the picture to my locker.

It had been taken at the Travoltas' Thanksgiving get-together. Me, running off, with Harlan's hand firmly attached to my arm and his mouth grinning lasciviously into the camera.

The caption: "America's latest 'Just Say No' poster girl, Morgan Carter, spent her Thanksgiving canoodling with hunky heartthrob Harlan Darly at a party hosted by John Travolta and Kelly Preston. Onlookers say that Carter dragged Darly into a nearby guest room for more 'privacy.' Wouldn't you like to have been a fly on *that* wall?"

How could I have not known about this shot?

Unless you were Marissa and knew the whole story, or Kirstie Alley, who got act three of the story all over her pretty gold pumps, you'd see this picture and think, "Hmmm, he's a little old for her, but look at Catherine Zeta-Jones and Michael Douglas. They're in love too."

I pulled the tear sheet off my locker door and crumpled it into a little ball. How the hell was I going to explain this to Eli without having to spill my whole history with Harlan? He was freaked out enough when it came to me and sex, so there was no possible way I could tell him I lost my virginity at age fourteen, to Harlan "I'm One of *People*'s 50 Most Beautiful People" Darly. He'd never be able to look at me again, let alone touch me.

"Hello, Morgan," I heard someone say, and when my eyes refocused, I realized that Debbie Ackerman was standing in front of me, a greasy, fake smile playing on her too-thin lips.

"What do you want?" I said.

"Oh, not much," she said back, all practiced casual. "But I did think you should know that I'm going to ask Eli to the Winter Wonderdance this afternoon."

I said, "Good luck with that. But I doubt that my *boyfriend* is going to accept your invitation to a dance that his twin sister—my best friend—is chairing."

She said, "I wouldn't be so certain."

I said, "I'm one hundred percent certain."

Debbie's greasy smile spread wider. "I don't know, Morgan. You were 'one hundred percent certain' that you were getting the lead in *Oklahoma!* too, and we all know how that turned out. Too bad all your money can't just, you know, *buy* Eli's affection for you."

I could literally feel every ounce of my blood pumping through my heart, and it took a whole lot of reserve not to deliver a right hook to her jaw. Instead, I took a step closer to her and bent down a bit so that we were eye to eye and in my coldest, bitchiest voice said, "Too bad there's not enough money in the world for your parents to buy *anyone's* affection for you. How's that diet of yours going, by the way? You might want to inform your ass that you're on one, because it doesn't seem to have gotten the message yet."

Then I turned on my heel and walked away as confidently as I could. Except I didn't feel confident. I felt awful. How could I, someone who's struggled with weight and body esteem issues all of my life, attack some poor chunky girl just because she threatened to steal my boyfriend?

Especially when said girl had zero chance of ever stealing said boyfriend?

I don't have much time to ponder this, however, because I just heard my name over the loudspeaker as Principal Barke called me to the office. I knew I'd get in trouble for skipping half a day yesterday, but now I'm worried about getting collared for the vandalism on Debbie's Jetta.

I thought maybe they'd just call Trudy or something and I'd get a stern talking-to. I have to say, I'm nervous. I've never once been in Principal Barke's office and had something good happen.

Eli was in the office when I arrived, looking as pale and pasty as he had when I told him that Emily wasn't as virginal as he assumed she was.

"Hey," I said. "I didn't hear them call you down."

"Don't," he said. "Not here."

"Don't what?" I asked.

He reached into his pocket and pulled out a folded square of cheap, glossy paper. I knew what was on the other side without even looking at it.

"Who gave that to you?" I asked.

He said, "Debbie Ackerman. It was waiting for me when I got home last night."

I said, "Why didn't you call me? I could've explained."

"Explained what?" he said morosely. "That you only have sex with other movie stars?"

It was the wrong thing to say, and I think he knew it too by the way he flinched as the words tumbled out of his mouth.

"Forget it," I said. "You think what you want. But I know what really happened, and it's not even close to what you think it is."

"I'm sure I should believe you," he said. "Just like I believed you about your dog-murdering psycho dad and your Pennsylvania Dutch upbringing."

I should've been angry. He had promised that we were starting over, a clean, blank slate. So why—*why?*—would he bring up stuff left over from "Claudia's" lies? And why was he so eager to assume that I was some kind of Hollywood whore instead of the mostly chaste girl I already told him I was?

But I was all out of anger. Instead, I sat down on a stiff blue guest chair, and I started to cry.

Eli didn't try to comfort me. He didn't get me a tissue, or ask me if I was okay, or even look at me with a soft sigh that let me know his heart hadn't turned into a rock. In fact, he took two steps away from me and asked the secretary—some new woman I'd never seen—if he could meet with Barke on his own.

Just then, Barke emerged from his brown wood-paneled office and called me and Eli in. Eli repeated his request, but Barke dismissed it immediately. Once we were all inside the office, Barke closed the door and said, "Miss Carter, would you care to explain to me why you were seen leaving campus after your lunch period yesterday, in your *limo*?"

I grabbed a tissue from the box on his desk and blew my nose into it, thankful that the Jetta had nothing to do with my being called into the office.

"Sure," I said, sniffling back what was left. "I got a crappy part in the school play, and I was feeling depressed."

"I thank you for your candor, Miss Carter," Barke said. Then he turned to Eli. "Would you care to offer an alternate version of Miss Carter's story? Something that involves a certain student's Jetta?"

"He didn't have anything to do with that," I said quickly.

"Miss Carter," Barke said, "I'm disappointed that you are unsatisfied with the role in which Ms. Bowman cast you. She was actually in my office several times before break, bragging about what a wonderful role she had for you and how you were going to make this year's production 'more than memorable.' Her words, by the way— 'more than memorable.' But I must say, I'm even more disappointed to find out that you really were involved in this act of vandalism."

"She wasn't," Eli said flatly. "It's like she said: she went home."

"And how do you know this, Mr. Whitmarsh?"

"Because I was there with her," he lied.

Why was Eli taking a bullet for me? Especially if he believed I'd actually had sex with Harlan when I was in California?

"Mr. Whitmarsh," Barke admonished, "I can't remember a single occasion of you breaking school rules. So I am hesitant to issue a punishment, especially on a first offense."

"Thank you, Mr. Barke," Eli said, all humble-like.

"I don't want to catch either of you truant ever again, do you understand me? Next time, I will not be so kind. Not only will your parents be called, but you will serve a full week of after-school detention."

"Wait a minute," I said. "You're not punishing *me*? But I've skipped school plenty of times before. So, what? That doesn't matter now?"

Barke said, "I'm confused, Miss Carter. Would you *like* me to punish you?"

"No," I said. "But I don't understand why you don't want to."

"Because," Eli explained, "if he gives you after-school detention, it will mess up your play rehearsal schedule."

"That's not my only consideration," Barke corrected. "But yes, I'd hate to see you fall behind with the play so early on."

"Fine," I said. "Can we go?"

"You may."

I wiped my eyes as I exited the office. Back in the hallway, I said to Eli, "I'm not sure why you just did that, but thank you."

"Don't," he said. "You and me—we're done."

Bile gathered at the back of my throat. "I should probably warn you that Debbie Ackerman is going to ask you to be her date for the Winter Wonderdance."

"Then I should probably warn you," he said coolly, "that I just might say yes."

I said, "Oh, that's mature. Lead on some girl who's been in love with you forever just to hurt my feelings."

"You don't have any problem hurting mine," he shot back.

"Maybe if you would listen to me," I said, "instead of pre-judging everything."

Eli suddenly stopped walking. "Look, Morgan—I don't want to get into this with you. We're done. Period. End of discussion."

At that exact moment, Riley appeared at the other end of the hallway, giving me a friendly wave. And I'm not sure what possessed me to do it, but I said to Eli, "You're right. We are." Then I strode down the hallway, dropped my back-pack on the floor, put my hands flat on Riley's face, and pressed my lips to his. People walking by started whistling and clapping, which gave me a sick sense of satisfaction, but I was sort of distracted by Riley's lack of enthusiasm for my unexpected kiss. I mean, after a few beats he started kissing me back, but his tongue moved around my mouth like a cold, dead sardine.

No one could be this bad a kisser, could they?

As we broke apart and I saw the shocked—and slightly concerned—look on Riley's face, I had this thought: Maybe he didn't want to be kissing *me*.

"I'm sorry," I said, my voice merely above a whisper.

"I don't know what to say," he replied. "Thank you?"

"Be my date to the Winter Wonderdance?" I blurted.

Riley sighed and reached his hand out to rub my shoulder. "What about Debbie?"

"She's already got a date," I said. I turned back toward Eli, who was already retreating down the hall.

"Oh," he said. "Okay. We'll go as friends."

"Just friends?" I said. "Not friends with potential?"

"No," he said. "You're on the rebound, toots. I don't want to get caught in the cross fire."

I nodded and said I understood, which I guess I did. Then he said, "I gotta run. But if you want to talk about it—why don't we grab coffee after rehearsal tomorrow? My treat."

"You had me at 'coffee,'" I said, smiling.

Riley grinned, reached up, and gave my cheek a little pinch—kind of like a Jewish grandmother might after calling you "bubbeleh."

"You're all right, toots," Riley said. "See you later."

The bell rang not ten seconds later, and there I was, standing in the hallway. I didn't feel like going to geometry or gym or even history, my favorite class. I certainly didn't feel like going to English, where I was sure to see Emily and get some kind of shit from her, either for my hallway stunt with Riley or for not having told her brother the truth about Harlan Darly to begin with.

I howled the f-word, right there in the hallway, just daring someone to give me detention or send me home for the day. But no one came.

So I picked up my backpack and slung it over my shoulder, walked out to the front parking lot, and called Thaddeus's beeper number. He dialed my cell thirty seconds later, and I asked him if he could pick me up from school. He didn't ask me why I wanted to go home in the middle of the day or offer any disapproval. I called him, and he came, and he took me home, where I could hide out and lick my deep, deep wounds.

11/30—Even later

When I got home, I called Sam to see what kind of spin control he was putting into action over the photos of me and Harlan together. Only Sam didn't see a need.

"This is good press for you, Morgan," he said. "Plus, Darly had me messenger an agency agreement over to him this afternoon. The plan worked!"

He told me he'd been given an advance copy of *EW*'s Hot List and that Brangelina were out while "Marlan" were in.

"Marlin?" I said. "Isn't that, like, a fish?"

"It's you," he explained. "Morgan and Harlan. Marlan. Isn't it fantastic?"

Then he gave me the name and number of Harlan's publicist. Apparently, I was to send all phone inquiries about our "romance" her way.

I hung up without saying goodbye.

I started to dial Marissa's cell but realized it was too early in the morning for her to be up. Goddamn these stupid time zones! I could've e-mailed. but Dotti would show her the gossip item soon enough. So I crawled back under the covers and tried to pretend this was all part of a bad dream. Only, I couldn't figure out when the dream went bad—like, was I going to have to back up all the way to the Viper Room?— so I got out my journal instead and here we are.

I have no idea what to do about school tomorrow. Do I go and act like nothing happened between me and Riley? What about Emily—how will this affect our friendship? And can I honestly do a table reading of *Oklahoma!* with everyone watching Debbie Ackerman lord it over me that she beat me out for the lead role?

Not to mention stole my boyfriend right out from under me?

Maybe I'll get lucky and Barke will suspend me for skipping school yet again.

11/30—Much later

Just got off the phone with Em. I guess she and I are okay, though she doesn't understand why I won't tell Eli about Harlan Darly.

"Trust me, Morgan," she kept saying. "He can handle that a lot better than thinking you ran off and hooked up with some Hollywood hunk."

I said, "You don't get it, Em. I need him to trust me. Instead, he just assumes that something terrible was going on. He never gave me the chance to explain, even when I asked for one."

She asked me about the rumor she heard—the one about me practically dry-humping Riley Augustine in the hallway.

"Oh, that," I said, trying to act like it was no big deal. "It was just . . . see . . . Well, Eli said he was going to the dance with Debbie Ackerman, so . . ."

"So you kissed Riley Augustine?" she finished for me.

"Something like that."

She said, "It's true then? You're taking Riley to the dance?"

"Yeah," I said. "I think I am."

Then Emily told me that she was too stressed to finish this conversation and that she needed to go get her DDR on before the arcade closed.

"One more thing," she said, before hanging up. "Did you tell my brother that Caspar and I were having sex?"

"Not really," I said. "Besides, you said Caspar announced it to the whole house!"

"Except that Eli wasn't there, you moron. Oh God," she groaned. "He won't even look me in the eye."

I said, "Welcome to my world," and then we hung up.

12/1

Let's review my social status at Snider High School up until this point:

- Started out the Invisible New Girl;
- Made a few friends and one frienemy (Debbie Ackerman, naturally) and became less invisible;
- Got active in VIP and became a little more visible; also had boy crushing on me big time;
- Was outed as undercover actress; suddenly most popular girl in school (for all the wrong reasons);
- Appeared on *Oprah*; another spike in popularity occured, even as supposed boyfriend ditched me at Casa d'Angelo;
- Made a new friend while fighting with the boyfriend, who was now an ex of sorts;
- Returned to Los Angeles and was congratulated on sobriety, but mostly walked around feeling like the girl who *used to be* Morgan Carter;
- Reunited with boy briefly before *People* magazine tagged Harlan Darly my newest conquest;

- Became branded a slut by the boy and ninety percent of the population at Snider H.S.;
- Came full circle; have returned to a state of invisibility, albeit for other reasons.

I'm in Bowman's class. When I walked in, she asked if I'd been sick the past two days and I said sort of, which isn't really a lie, because you can be sick with grief. It's, like, medically proven or whatever. Then she was quick to make sure I'd be at rehearsal after school for the table read. I assured her that I would be, although I asked if I could talk to her for a few minutes before rehearsal officially begins.

Last bell is in five. Am looking forward to confronting Bowman about her poor choice in casting.

12/1—*Later*

So, I chickened out. But I had good reason. See, I waited until Bowman's classroom was clear before approaching her about being cast as slutty Annie instead of virginal Laurey, and her eyes widened all sincere-like and she said, "But Morgan, I never in a million years thought you'd want to play Laurey. I mean, she's almost annoying in her prissiness. Annie seemed like a meatier role in general—you'll even get to do some physical comedy!"

It is hard to argue with someone who screwed up without realizing she screwed up, but I tried to make my point anyway.

"Physical comedy is good, yes. But Ms. Bowman—you may not know this, but for whatever reason, I don't have the most spotless reputation around here. It's all just rumors, of course, but . . . well . . . playing Annie—the town whore? I mean, you can see where that might come back on a person."

"Let me get this straight," she said. "You, Morgan Carter, an Oscar-nominated actress—you're upset because some local girls are giving you a hard time out of what? Jealousy? Insecurity? You've been tabloid fodder since you were ten years old, my dear. Do you really want to run scared from a couple of mean girls and some gossip-hungry newspaper reporters?"

When she put it that way, I lost the rest of my words. Partly because she was right and partly because . . .

Okay, fine. She was one hundred percent right, and I was being a total idiot.

"Fine," I said. "But I'm giving Annie some brains too. She can't really be as dumb as the script says."

"I'll do you one better," Ms. B said. "What would you think if I told you we were doing *Oklahoma!* in modern dress, as an allegory of sorts? Where Ado Annie dresses like Britney Spears and every time you make an entrance, there's a musical cue from one of Britney's songs?"

All of the synapses in my brain fired off as I tried to contemplate the possibilities. "It's a commentary," I said, "on the conflicting messages today's teens get in terms of social mores. Right?"

"See?" Ms. Bowman smiled brightly. "This Annie's already gotten brainier."

Barke will flip his shit when he sees what Bowman's got planned, but I have to say: she's my new favorite teacher. She may even rival Ms. Janet Moore for my scholastic affection.

12/1—*Even later*

Table reading went well. Debbie looked puzzled when Ms. Bowman told us we wouldn't be using accents and that at the table read, we should be ourselves and not try to act. I was fine with it—it's pretty standard, especially on TV—but everyone else was having a hard time not being the character they were supposed to be playing.

Just as I was heading out, Debbie tried to get me fired up by making some crude comment about the costume designer needing to keep really good track of Will's and my underwear (Will being Riley, of course), but I didn't give her the satisfaction of reacting. Instead, I just smiled and told her I'd see her tomorrow for the first sing-through.

So, things still suck for the most part, but I'll survive.

I always do.

12/2

I might have spoken too soon about that surviving thing.

See, I thought things couldn't get any worse. Eli continues to ignore me, Emily continues to bug me about telling him the truth, and Riley's sending me mixed signals.

For example: he was flirty with me at rehearsal and asked me if I wanted to grab that cup of coffee and talk. I ld him I had to be at my meeting by seven and he said he'd more than happy to drive me there and even stay with I wanted him to. Which is nice, right?

ve go to Starbucks, and he picks up the tab, and then to my meeting with me, and in the middle of -four-hundred-pound-recovering-heroin-addict's ches over and takes my hand and gives it a little squeeze. It's a sweet gesture, something I might expect of Eli but not necessarily Riley.

Then everything goes to shit.

Gabby, the facilitator, asks if there are any new members who'd like to introduce themselves. A hand shoots up in the back of the room; a tall, buffed-out body follows.

"Hi," I hear him say, in that slow, drawling voice. "I'm Harlan, and I'm a recovering alcoholic and addict."

Suddenly, all eyes are Ping-Ponging between me and Harlan. Even Riley's eyes are bugging out of his head.

Harlan gives me a little wave, all smiles and dimples. Time freezes as I realize that there's absolutely no place on earth where I am safe from the evil that is Harlan Darly. I mean, what the hell was he doing in *my* meeting? Here, in Fort Wayne?

"Riley," I said in a hoarse whisper. "Please take me home now."

We'd started to head toward the exit when I heard Harlan call out, "Morgan, wait!" I broke into a sprint; Riley matched my pace.

"Open the door!" I said, panicked.

He does, and we spring into his car. I'm yelling, "Go, go, go!" before either of us has our seat belts fastened, and Riley takes off so quickly he leaves rubber behind.

"Uh, Morgan?" he asks when we're at least two miles from the school. "Can you tell me why you're on the run from Harlan Darly?"

"No," I said.

Hey, I wanted to be honest, and honestly—I couldn't tell him.

"Okay," Riley said, turning on the radio.

He dropped the subject so quickly that I was surprised.

"Aren't you going to ask me again?"

"Do you want me to ask you again?"

"No."

He nodded. "So I won't. If you wanted me to know, you'd tell me. Right?"

I was quiet for a minute. Then I realize how big this gift is that Riley's given me.

"Thank you," I said.

"Not a problem."

I spent the rest of the night holed up in the house, jumping every time I saw car lights beaming through the window sheers. I was so terrified Harlan was going to show up at the front door. What was I going to say? What was I going to do? And why—*why*—was he even here?

Except I already knew the answer to that one.

12/2—Later

Trudy thought we needed to call the police and get a detail put on the house, but I said, "They're not going to do that. I can't file a restraining order against him—at least not until I can prove that he's stalking me."

"He's here, isn't he?" she said. "Isn't that proof enough?"

"For me and you, yeah. But to the police? I mean, Jesus, Tru—the papers are saying that I'm the love of his life and that we hooked up when I went home. We're *Marlan*, for Christ's sake. Everyone will just think that he's trying to woo me."

Even so, Trudy checked the locks on all the windows and doors before going to bed. Then she made me promise to wake her up if Harlan actually showed.

It's way past midnight now.

Except neither of us seem to be getting any sleep tonight.

12/3

I should've known.

He was waiting for me on the front steps, holding a dozen red roses, when Thaddeus pulled up to the curb at Snider High. Half the student body was standing around him but like three feet away, so there was this small force field of "no touch" surrounding his body.

I almost—almost—didn't get out of the car.

But then he saved me.

Riley.

He bounded down the steps, pushing through a throng of fellow students until he reached the door to the limo. He knocked on the window twice, and I slowly opened the door. Riley slipped his arm through mine and said, "Let's go, toots."

I saw anger flash across Harlan's face; after all, Riley had stolen his moment. But then he remembered the part he was supposed to play and wiped the anger away, replacing it with sadness, complete with pleading eyes and wrinkled forehead.

"Morgan!" he said. "Please, let's just talk! Please!"

"She's busy," Riley informed him, steering me toward the door.

Harlan got all up in his grill and said, "Go away, queer boy. This has nothing to do with you." Then he pushed him aside with the back of his hand, as though he were garbage. Riley bounced off the glass of the door.

I whirled on Darly. "Leave him alone!" I screamed. "You can't talk to my friends that way! And you can't talk to me. Ever!"

197

I grabbed Harlan by the arm, hard, and dragged him into the front office, where I told Barke's secretary that I needed to use *his* office for something very important. She looked at me like I was high. Then, reluctantly, she unlocked Barke's door and I pulled Harlan in after me.

"This has got to stop," I said firmly. "You need to tell everyone that our entire 'relationship' is a joke. A really stupid joke."

"No way," he drawled. "My Q rating is through the roof. And it's all because of you, my little honey bunny." He tossed the roses onto Barke's desk.

"You'll do it," I said, my voice almost a growl. "And you'll do it today."

"Or what?" he challenged.

I had reached my breaking point. "Or I'm going to tell everyone what happened between us."

He laughed. "What? That you dragged me into a bathroom, then hid in a shower stall?"

"No," I said, pulling strength from God-knows-where. "I mean, I'll tell them what happened three years ago."

His face wrinkled up as he did the math. "What happened three years ago?"

I might have expected him to say something like, "What, when we slept together?"

But this? This was *wrong*. He didn't even *remember*.

In a few short steps, I was standing straight in front of him. Then, without another thought, I slapped him across the face. Hard.

A stream of obscenities escaped Harlan's lips. "What the hell is your problem?" he spat.

"My problem," I said coolly, "is that you raped me. Three

198

years ago. In your trailer. You got me drunk, you got me high, and then you raped me. I was fourteen years old. I was a *virgin*. And you, you piece of shit—you *raped* me."

He shrugged and said, "You can't prove anything."

His words hit as hard as if he'd slapped me back. "That's all you have to say? I can't prove that it happened?"

"Shit," he said, "I was wasted most of that year. And if memory serves, you were too, darlin'."

It was the "darlin'" that did me in. With Marissa's words echoing in my ears, I lifted my knee and jammed it into the soft flesh of his pathetic package.

Harlan instantly crumpled to the floor, howling in pain.

I said, "Don't worry, *darlin'*. I don't need to prove anything to anybody. Your disgusting secret is safe with me."

I left him there, lying fetal on the floor of Barke's office, and felt a surge of energy. I'd faced the demon, and I'd *won*. But then, just as quickly, the sweet taste of victory turned sour.

To the world outside, nothing had changed. So what, exactly, had I won?

Riley was sitting in the office lobby, waiting for me I guess. "You okay?" he asked.

I nodded. "Let's get out of here."

We took his car because it was less conspicuous than the limo and drove to Starbucks. Instead of drinking our coffees there, we got back in his car. Riley started driving around aimlessly, not saying anything, until he pulled into the parking lot of a Kroger and cut the engine.

"I'm sorry," I told him. "I'm sorry for that scene this morning. And I'm sorry for what he said to you."

"Morgan—" Riley started.

But I couldn't let him finish. My blood pressure soared

just thinking about it. "I mean, Jesus Christ, where does he come off saying that you're—"

"Morgan," Riley interrupted. "I'm gay."

I shook my head, trying to process this.

"Riley, it's totally cool that you don't want to date me. I probably wouldn't want to date me either. But you don't have to pretend to be gay just to get rid of me. I do know how to take no for an answer."

"I'm not pretending," he said quietly. "I really am gay."

"But—but your privates wanted to have a conversation with my privates," I protested.

"Yeah," he said. "But you know, you're not the only one I've said that to."

"Ouch," I said. "You really know how to make a girl feel special."

But Riley didn't smile. "I do it so no one will ask too many questions."

I am stunned speechless when he says this. The pieces of the puzzle begin to slide together. He's into musical theater. He's an excellent dancer. He fully spends a lot of free time at the gym. He knows how to dress. He's a good listener.

He kissed me like a dead fish. He *is* gay.

"You knew," he says, breaking my train of thought. "That day in the hallway, when you kissed me. I could see it in your eyes."

"No," I protest. "I didn't."

"Yeah, you did," he says. "You just didn't know you knew. But you would've figured it out eventually."

I chug the rest of my grande Sumatra. "Man, being this far from Hollywood has really screwed with my gay-dar. But why are you telling *me* this?"

"I guess—it's because of yesterday. Being at your meeting with you. You're so brave, Morgan. I'm not that brave. At least, not yet.

And then he started to cry, just a little, but it was enough to get me all choked up. I took a Starbucks napkin and handed it to him, and as he blew his nose, it honked a bit and we both laughed.

"Jesus." I shook my head. "I guess I'm somebody's hag."

Riley grinned. "I prefer the term 'beard' myself."

"I won't tell anyone," I promised him. "You can trust me."

"I know that," he said. "I wouldn't have told you if I didn't."

Then I go, "I'm not as brave as you think I am."

"Why do you say that?"

"Because all I did was knee him in the balls."

Riley choked on his coffee. "Harlan Darly?" he asks. "That's what you were doing in Barke's office?"

"If I was really brave," I said, "I wouldn't have told him I'd keep his dirty secret."

"Keep what a secret?"

I tried to see myself as Riley saw me—someone brave. I drained the rest of my grande Sumatra and sighed.

"It's all fake, the tabloid stuff," I confessed. "Harlan's not heartbroken over me. He doesn't even have a heart, as far as I know. It's all a big publicity stunt—orchestrated by my manager."

"That sucks," Riley says. "But how does that make you not brave?"

"Let me finish." I went to take another gulp of coffee before realizing my cup was empty. So I took Riley's and drained his cup too.

"Three years ago, Harlan Darly and I were doing a movie together. I had this enormous crush on him. I was drinking then and smoking up, and one night, in his trailer, he . . ."

"No," Riley said. "Don't tell me that."

I nodded. "It's true. I never told anyone. I mean, now people know. A few people. Three, to be exact. Well, including you, there's four—"

Riley sighed and pulled me close to him. "I'm really sorry, Morgan. I had a good friend back in Chicago who had the same thing happen to her. Except the guy was, like, some band geek, instead of a movie star.

"She was really messed up over it," he went on. "And she never reported it either. But you know what? That doesn't make her chicken. And it doesn't make you any less brave."

I wanted to believe him—needed to—but everything was happening so fast. I felt like just yesterday Eli was showing me how to pack my suitcase to maximize space. And now . . . Harlan Darly was here, in Fort Wayne.

It was like there was no safe place anymore. No place I could hide from my problems.

Riley started the car. "Home?" he asked.

Yeah. If only I knew where that was.

12/4

Just got off the phone with a most unexpected caller: Ms. Janet Moore.

It was like she could read my mind, because she called when I should've been in chemistry class getting my ass chewed out by An-Yi. She told me she had this feeling that I needed to talk to her and she thought she'd leave a message for me.

"I'm not sure I want to know why you're not in school," she said, "but it does sound like I was right. So what's up? How are you doing?"

So I spilled it all—the troubles with Eli, how everyone keeps assuming I'm some sort of skank, Harlan Darly show-ing up and me confronting him in Barke's office—I told her everything except the part about Riley being gay because I promised him I wouldn't tell anyone and I meant it.

"Oh, Morgan," she said. "How are you holding up?"

"Okay," I said. "I mean, I'm still a little shell-shocked, what with Harlan showing up here and all. And it sucks about Eli, but if he's not going to trust me, then what else is there? I feel like he wants to believe the worst about me."

"He probably does," she said. "It's safer that way. If he rejects you before you reject him, then in some twisted way, he's protecting himself.

"But you know what?" she continued. "I've heard a lot about Eli, and I think he'll come around. Just give him some time. Let him figure it out for himself. He's a smart boy; eventually he'll realize that his backward ways of protecting himself are really just cutting him off from the good things that life has to offer."

Then she said, "I can't tell you how proud I am of you for confronting Harlan. I hope—I really, really hope—that this helps you heal some."

"Yeah," I said. "Me, too."

I told her that I missed her fiercely and that I wished she'd come back.

"Never!" she said, laughing. "It's gorgeous out here. You should think about coming to visit—maybe over your spring break?"

"Would you let me?" I asked, and she said, "I'd love to see you again. Honestly."

Before we hung up, she told me I should read this article that's in the new issue of *People*. She said I'd find it relevant to some of the stuff I was dealing with. So, I guess I'll go do that now.

12/4—*Later*

Ms. Janet Moore is the bomb. That article she told me to read? It was about how women need to stop calling each other sluts and whores, even jokingly, because it perpetuates the stereotype that female sexuality is somehow bad. It's different, the author said, than gays reappropriating "queer," because queer has become a symbol of pride. Whereas we still use words like *bitch* as really derogatory, so to use them in fun is to tell men it's okay for them to call us that too.

So I've been thinking. I've been thinking about how girls like Debbie Ackerman don't think twice about spreading baseless rumors about girls like me. I've been thinking about how Eli went from seeing me as a fragile goddess creature to some Hollywood whore all because of the trash I've allowed tabloids to talk about me for as long as I can remember.

And then I started thinking about how I could make it stop. Or at least do something positive to try and put a stop to it.

What I did was this:

I made a bunch of calls, and I got the number of the reporter who wrote that story in *People*. And then I made some more calls until I got this Susan Pettit on her cell. She was at her nephew's birthday party and asked me if I could hold on until after they sang to him. I said okay, and when she came back, I told her how much I appreciated her article and how brilliant I thought she was.

She said, "That's, uh, really flattering and all. But, uh, why did you have to track me down today?"

I told her that if I hadn't done it today, I was afraid I'd lose my nerve. Then I said, "How would you like a big, fat, exclusive scoop?"

"Sure," she said. "What is it?"

I swallowed hard and told myself I could still back out. I could hang up the phone and become some sort of bizarre anecdote this reporter dragged out at Christmas parties and family functions.

But no. I'd been silent for way too long.

It was time to find my voice.

It was time to be truly brave.

"Three years ago," I began, "I was raped. I was a virgin and I was raped by someone really famous, and I didn't do anything about it because I was using drugs, even back then. But what he did was wrong, and I need to set the record straight."

"Oh my God," Susan said. "I'm really sorry to hear that."

"Thanks," I said.

Then she said, "This might sound cold, but . . . do you have anyone who could back up your story?"

"No," I told her honestly. "Like I said, I never told anyone. Not until last year, but that was just my counselor. So here's what I'm thinking. We won't name names. I'll tell my story, leaving out just enough details so as not to identify my rapist. He'll know it's about him, and people will speculate, but you won't get in any trouble."

She told me she needed to call her editor and run it by the legal department first.

"That's fine," I said. "But there's one stipulation. It has to come out in next week's issue or the deal is off the table."

"I can't promise that," she said. "There are protocols—stories have already been slotted."

"But you're a weekly magazine," I said. "If you could run a cover story about Britney's marriage with less than twenty-four hours' notice, I think you could find a way to get me into next Monday's issue."

Susan called me back an hour later and said we were on, but she was getting crap from her family about missing the party and could she call me back in another hour? I told her sure, and she should be calling any minute.

12/4—*Much, much later*

Six hours on the phone, but it's done. It will be in Monday's issue. The headline will even be on the cover. Susan's editor decided to run with it as a first-person account—one of those "as told to" pieces.

I told Trudy already, and she was shocked but very supportive. She told me that I should probably call Sam and Bianca by tomorrow night, because it wasn't fair to let them find out with the rest of the world.

I think she's right.

Feeling beyond exhausted now. Will try to get some sleep before making the hardest phone call I've ever had to make.

12/5

Woke up with a stomachache, thinking, *I shouldn't have done that*. But I did. And now it's too late. Which is a good thing, I think, because even if I feel a little morning-after regret, in the long run, this will be a good thing. This will help set me free.

And then I called my mother.

I don't remember a lot of what was said, but I can't get the sound of my mother's sobs out of my ears. "Why?" she cried over and over. "Why didn't you tell me? I am your mother. I could've protected you."

Sam's reaction was way less dramatic but no less concerned. "Are you sure you want to go public with this?"

"Yes," I said. "I should've done it years ago."

"Why now?" he asked.

I hesitated for a minute, then said, "Promise me you won't do anything drastic."

"Okay," he agreed.

"Harlan Darly."

"What?"

"Harlan Darly," I repeated. "He's the one."

I could hear Sam's sharp intake of breath through the phone. Then he said, "I want to kill that bastard."

"You don't have to do that," I said. "I'm . . . making my peace with it."

"Okay, so I won't kill him. I'll just, you know, kill his career," he said. "And I will take great pleasure in destroying him."

I was quiet for a minute. Then I said, "I'm going to be accused of making it up, you know. Especially since I wouldn't name names and I won't confirm any guesses. People will say it's another publicity stunt."

"I know, sweetheart," he said. "I've been in this business a lot longer than you. Whatever they throw at you, we can handle. I'm here for you a hundred percent."

"Even if it means giving up your new client?"

Sam sighed. "My business will survive without Harlan Darly. I just wish . . . I wish you'd told me sooner, kiddo. I feel awful. What you must've been going through these past few weeks—these past few years . . ."

"Don't," I said. "It's not your fault. Not telling . . . that was my way of trying to protect you. I just couldn't disappoint you again."

"Oh, honey," he said. "I love you. And please don't ever think I'm disappointed in you. I couldn't be more proud of you if you were my own flesh and blood."

Then he told me that if I wanted to come home at all—even for the weekend—I should just say the word and he'd get a ticket out to me ASAP.

"Go console your wife," I said. "I think she needs you more than I do right now."

12/5—Later

If Susan Pettit is a woman of her word, a preview of the *People* story should be leaked to the *Journal Gazette* and *News-Sentinel* in just enough time for them to beat the morning press but not early enough for *People* to lose their scoop.

Trudy canceled her date with Dave to sit home with me tonight. My stomach is in knots, so much so that I can't even eat the beautiful-smelling kung pao beef that T. ordered for my dinner. I can barely choke down the herbal tea she brewed for me hours ago to help settle my nerves.

I debated whether or not I should call Em and give her a heads-up, but I didn't want her to be the one to tell Eli. For some reason, that feels really important to me.

Tomorrow can't come soon enough.

12/6

I made the front page of both newspapers AND *People* magazine. They used an old photo of me, one that was taken while I was high off my ass and everyone knew it but no one was doing anything to stop me. In the picture, I am fourteen—the same age I was when Harlan Darly raped me.

Susan knows it was him. I had to tell her so she could tell the legal department so that there would be nothing in the article that would definitively identify him. With nothing but my word, it would be very easy for him to sue for libel. But my guess is that I'm not the first girl Harlan Darly took advantage of. If he ever went public, I'm almost positive there'd be a string of girls seeping out of the woodwork, corroborating my story because it happened to them too.

School has been weird. Lots of people staring at me, lots of others unable to look me in the eye. A few brave souls asked me if it was true, and a few idiots asked me who "hit that." Meaning me, of course. My teachers have been giving me sympathetic smiles and stopping me after class to assure me they're there if I need to talk.

It makes me feel slightly queasy, because pity is that last thing I'm looking for right now.

I didn't see Em until English, and the first thing she did was throw her arms around me in a hug.

"I can't believe you did it!" she said. "You're like . . . you're my hero."

"I need a favor," I said. "Can we go off campus for lunch? Even if we just drive around the block for half an hour? I don't think I could deal with the caf today."

"Not a problem."

We went through the McDonald's drive-through, then ate in the parking lot. Em asked a few tentative questions, and I told her about how Susan's article had inspired me to speak up.

Then I said, "Does Eli know?"

"I don't know," Em said, shrugging. "I haven't seen him since we got to school. I didn't find out until homeroom."

We ran into Riley when got back. He was pacing the front of the building like an expectant dad. When he saw me, he threw his arms around my waist and lifted me up, practically whooping.

"You've got a bigger pair than I do, Morgan Carter," he said. "You are a princess. No! You're a *queen*."

"I'm in good company," I whispered in his ear, and he grinned.

Then I said, "Tell me you didn't get a chance to start phase three." He told me he hadn't.

"Good," I said. "I want to abort the mission."

"Yeah? Why the change of heart?"

"Because I don't need it anymore," I said. "Don't get me wrong—I still think Debbie's a horrible person—but it's not up to me to give her payback. I'll leave that up to karma."

The rest of the day passed by in a blur. Trudy got off work early and picked me up after play rehearsal, and we drove to the Cracker Barrel and ordered a lot of food that will most likely clog our arteries. It felt kind of good, actually. Not the artery-clogging part but the part about me and Trudy out for dinner, just two old girls taking pleasure in each other's company.

And then we got home, and I saw the Camry before I saw him sitting on the front stoop, cold and forlorn. It was Eli, his cheeks blistered by wintry winds. Before Trudy could even get the key in the lock he said, "It was him, wasn't it? The guy from the picture. The one who showed up at school the other day."

I nodded.

And then he said, his voice full of angst, "Why didn't you just tell me?"

"Because," I said, "I didn't want to have to."

Trudy said it was too cold for us to be having this conversation outside, so we moved into the living room and she excused herself to the bedroom to go call Dave. I asked Eli if he wanted me to make some coffee and he said no.

"I feel like an ass," he said.

"Good," I said. "You've been acting like one."

He didn't have a response to that.

After a while, I said, "It wouldn't have mattered much if I'd told you about me and Harlan Darly. I mean, maybe it would have bought us some more time. But when it comes to me, Eli, you've got some serious issues. And I can't say I blame you, exactly. I'm just sad you can't get past them."

"But we can," he said. "We just need a do-over."

"We already had one of those," I reminded him. "It didn't go so well."

He goes, "That's because you weren't fully honest."

"Uh-uh." I shook my head. "I asked you to let me explain, but your mind was already made up. And like I said—I didn't want to have to explain. I wanted you to believe me when I said it wasn't what it looked like. You're not ready to do that. So okay. Good to know."

He sat silent for a while, and then he said, "So it's over? For good?"

"Well, Eli," I replied, "I don't think it ever really got started. I'm sorry. I think . . . I think I'm better off alone right now."

He nodded and stood up from the couch. "For what it's worth, I'm sorry too."

"I know you are," I said.

Eli asked if he could hug me, and I said okay, even though I wasn't sure it was, and when he let go, it was really, really hard to watch him walk away. But I think Ms. Janet Moore is right. I think I need to give him time and space. And then, if it's meant to be, it'll happen.

Trudy's calling me from the other room—something about too many messages on the answering machine. . . .

12/6—Later

Oh my God. We have more than fifty messages, all of them about me and the story in *People*. All asking for exclusive on-air interviews or in-depth print stuff. There were more coming in, too, when Trudy was trying to talk to Dave. After Eli left, she brought out a list ten numbers long, and then we sat down to listen to all of the ones on the machine. We'd barely gotten through six when the phone rang again. Trudy picked it up for me.

"Yes," she said, "she's right here." She handed me the phone.

It was Diane Sawyer.

She was looking for an exclusive like everyone else, but I

told her I didn't really feel like doing any more press. "I already told my story," I said. "But thank you for calling."

"Hold on a second, Morgan," Diane said. "I'd love to get that exclusive with you, but if I don't, so be it. However, it would be a sin if you decided you weren't going to talk to anyone on air. Television is a powerful medium, and you, young lady, have a powerful, important story to tell.

"You might be a Hollywood starlet," she continued, "but you're also just a girl. A normal, teenage girl. Think of how many people you could help by talking about everything you've been through. How many girls, just like you, who abuse drugs and alcohol because they're in so much pain and can't find a way out. And how many of those girls, like you, end up being abused by some guy.

"Tell your story, Morgan. If not to me, then to someone."

After a speech like that, how could I say no?

So Diane is flying out tomorrow to do the interview, and I told Sam if *Oprah* calls, I'll do her show again too. Because I *do* want to help. Even if it means I'm exposing myself to more criticism.

All I really want right now is to finish my junior year in peace. I know that sounds kind of dumb, but it's been a hard ride, transitioning to life in the Fort. I've worked really hard to get where I am, and I've had to put up with a lot of crap along the way. Plus, now it's like this thing I need to prove to myself. That I can do it. That I can survive a year as a normal teenage girl.

After all, I'm already halfway there.

12/18

Long time, no write.

That's because I didn't have you. See, right after the *People* story broke, Sam got a call from a very important editor at a very important publishing house in New York City. And she told him she wanted me to write a book about my life. It wasn't the first call like this that he's fielded since my outing last October, but what struck him about this editor in particular was that she wasn't talking about film rights or fictionalizing things or hiring a ghostwriter to do all the work.

She said, "I've heard rumors of a diary. I'd like to publish that."

So Sam had her call me, and we talked, and I liked this woman a lot. She told me that I could set the pace, that they wouldn't publish anything I didn't want published, and that they only wanted me to tell my story. No one else. Just me.

Sam drew up some agreement that temporarily protected my rights to the material, and I sent my two journals to the New York editor. Meanwhile, Sam got me this awesome literary agent. His name is George, and he's some kind of publishing legend. He sounds like a really nice grandpa on the phone, and I think I'm going to like working with him lots.

Anyway, I just got my journals back today. Kristen, my editor, told me they made her cry several times. Then she said she was talking to George about me coming to New York over Christmas break so she and I could work on the editing together. They're hiring a woman to type up all my entries and everything! And then they're going to rush to get the book out by August so I can do some promotion before school starts up again.

For some reason, that was important to me. School starting up, I mean. I think I want to finish high school here in Fort Wayne. It seems . . . I don't know. Right? It's just something I want to do.

Gotta wrap this up. Tonight is the Winter Wonderdance, and I'm going to get to wear my beautiful blue velvet dress and dance on the arm of a dashing young man.

12/18 — *Later*

The Winter Wonderdance was perfect. Absolutely perfect! Riley was a total gentleman. Emily wore this sexy red getup and brought Caspar as her date. LaTanya showed up with Luke Paxton on her arm, and I just about *died*. Meadow Forrester brought Colin McAfee as her date, and me and LaTanya debated as to whether or not Meadow knew that Colin was actually gay and liked having him as her default date or if she was secretly in love with him and hoping to turn him back to the home team.

I felt a little self-conscious discussing this around Riley, but he gave me a secret wink to let me know it was okay.

We took turns getting our pictures taken under an arbor of holly, with a picture of Santa and some reindeer as a backdrop. Political correctness has so far evaded my high school, as there wasn't a single menorah or mention of Kwanzaa to be seen.

And then I asked the DJ if he would play "That's What Friends Are For," and he told me it was so old that he didn't think he had it in his collection anymore. So then I asked him if he had the Beatles' "In My Life," and he said, "What do you think?" He didn't even have Ben E. King's "Stand by Me."

"What the hell kind of DJ are you, anyway?" I growled.

He shrugged. "I think I have a rap version of 'Lean on Me' somewhere in that box."

So I dug through the box and pulled out the CD and told him to play it. Then I ran back onto the dance floor, pulling off my shoes, and herded all of my friends into a big circle. "LaTanya!" I yelled over the music. "Help me sing it, will you?"

We stood there, our arms over each other's shoulders, swaying back and forth. Emily and Riley joined me and LaTanya with the singing part, and pretty soon Meadow and Colin were busting into our circle and singing along with us. By the end of the song, there were like twenty of us shouting lyrics to each other, and I was so happy I didn't even notice there were tears running down my cheeks.

It was a cheesy teen movie moment, but it was mine.

I felt like a typical midwestern teenager. *Finally*.

When the song ended, Emily hugged me and told me she loved me, and I told her I loved her too.

And that's when Eli arrived.

The whole scene was very *Pretty in Pink*—you know, the part when Andrew McCarthy shows up at the prom and tells Molly Ringwald he loves her and then walks away and Ducky tells her to go after him? Well, Eli was my Andrew McCarthy, and Riley was my Ducky (except I don't think Ducky was really gay—he just sort of dressed gay) and anyway, what happened was this:

We ended up standing on the front steps of school. It was snowing, a light, powdery snow, and the wind was making it fly around like solid pixie dust.

"I miss you," Eli said, and I told him I missed him too.

He congratulated me on my book deal—I guess Em had told

him—and he said, "Just don't make me look too bad, okay?"

"I don't think you're bad," I said. "I've never thought that."

Then Eli reached into his pocket and pulled out a little square-shaped package wrapped in silver paper. "An early Christmas present," he said, handing it to me.

I opened it and found a black velvet jewelry box—the kind that engagement rings come in. Only, inside this one was a small circle pendant. On the front of it was a tiny engraved triangle, and on the back were engraved the words *One Day at a Time*.

"How did you know?" I asked, looking up and into his shining eyes.

"Research," he said. "I wanted to get you something meaningful, so I Googled Alcoholics Anonymous and found out that was the motto. It seemed fitting somehow for us too. Like, maybe if we had taken things one day at a time, they would've worked out differently."

"Yeah," I said. "Maybe."

And then he leaned in like he was going to kiss me, but I turned away so that his lips landed behind my left ear.

"I'll be better," Eli whispered. "I promise."

"No promises," I whispered back. "Let's just take it one day at a time."

Well, I'm out of pages now, and Kristen wants me to make notes about what to leave out so that the typist can get started. I guess it's sort of appropriate. I'm starting another new chapter in my life, so why wouldn't I want to start with a blank book, on a blank page?

I don't know what the future holds, but I'm happy living in the now.